"The Cure for Robot Cancer"
By Uncle Mikey

©2021 Michael Gipson Leavitt
Vashon, WA USA
MikeLeavittArt.com

The Cure for Robot Cancer

Mechanical infections fester. Little bits of machinery grow inside body parts. It passes between people through vapor and secretions. Growing voraciously like tumors, it's nicknamed a "cancer". Small pieces of metal, pipes, hoses or circuitry form on (or in) your body when you come within ten feet of someone afflicted with the digital disease. The use of electronics creates host environments that encourage growth. Each human slowly becomes a cyborg. Many are completely subsumed in electronics. Some turn into CPU's. Others become programmable washing machines, jet skies, Dysons or automatic coffee makers. More than twenty years into the twenty-first century, the original infection is unknown.
The cure is unknown.

Many go "back to the Earth." They shut down all digital devices, turn off every machine, and discard each mechanical unit they own. This effort fails.

And so, after the desperately long years of a rapidly mechanizing world, non-linear proposals are finally heard. You might not think a poet would find an actual escape. You definitely wouldn't expect it from the brooding poetry of a moody teenager, that's for damn sure. No, science only applies when humans unilaterally agree on how to change their behavior. Sometimes a concrete solution comes the old-fashioned, medieval way.

The instructions to defeat robot cancer (as it becomes known) come from nowhere. There isn't even a hero. There are two of them. The mechanical infections drive them apart. Love brings all back together. Twenty-one moons is all it took.

This is the story of Cat and Wolf, two kids with a love so deep and wide that it spans the solar system to cure a plague.

Can their experiment be replicated? Well, this is an instructional manual, of sorts. The way to find out is by reading on. The cure is just a howl away.

So, to let others speak for themselves, we will let our heroes spin their own yarn. Here is the story of Cat and Wolf, told in their own words, alternating their parts in the story so as not to step on each others' toes.

1

Cat's Tale

Wolves like packs and cats like to be alone, right? So wolves don't normally get along with cats, right? Well, I say humans don't get along with each other either. Because if something infecting the whole planet couldn't bring us together, nothing could.

This particular cat grew intensely close to one wolf. Then we got pushed apart, about as far apart as we could go. Then we came back together and saved the world. And it was our reunion that got everyone to agree on one thing.

It wasn't a disease of the body. It was a disease of the mind. The cure wasn't in a lab. It came from deep down inside, from the place where all the best ideas and greatest decisions are ever made. You know how - when you suggest an idea to someone who doesn't want to hear it, then days later they suggest the same idea as if you'd never suggested it? *That's* the place where the cure for robot cancer came from.

It dawned on me one day while pawing my Wolf, "We're going to have to save ourselves."

She stopped eating lunch. "We can't do it by ourselves, Cat."

I was indignant, "Look around, babe. These people have no freaking clue."

"78 more deaths, er, transmutations to report today due to the digital infections," the TV news guy reported to the crowded luncheonette quietly watching. "That brings our total to 59,000 mutations and nearly 300,00 reported infections in the last two weeks, since the first reported case."

Everyone in the diner kept eating.

The TV kept blaring, "We must use this as a friendly reminder to not go indoors out in public, and, please, do not frequent establishments with more than one other person in attendance. Officials remind us to stay ten feet apart. Remember: your breath and touch are lethal."

Forks, knives, spoons, plates and tables of the busy restaurant kept on clanking away. No one said a word. No one got up and left. No one wondered if it was someone they knew at that point. They just continued eating and watching the TV.

"Check, please," Wolf chirped.

I laid down a twenty and five. "That'll cover tip. Let's jet." We left without looking back.

Wolf and I met in class a little more than three years before that luncheonette day. It was one of those typical days to reminisce from the "before" times. Our introduction happened like a billion other kids a billion times before. There was no secret note passed, no awkward call to attention, not even a magical spark.

Her friend Kate introduced us, "Wolf, this is Cat." She was sitting right in front of me.

I was into Kate. So I only acted like I was into Wolf at first, just enough to get Kate's attention. I figured, *"If I'm nice to this new friend, Kate might like me more… Kate and Cat!"* I liked the sound of it.

I greeted her politely, "Nice to meet you, Wolf." We held eye contact, but Kate was the shiny object. I was falling for the lure. I couldn't get around Wolf's braces, which was totally hypocritical because my mouth, too, was laden with them. Two mouths intertwined with stainless steel and rubber bands were separated by the three feet between our formica school desks.

"EYES UP FRONT," Mr. Rosvik shot into our trio. I paid him no mind. He was a middle-aged gay man. I knew he liked me. I knew I had Mr. Rosvik in my back pocket. I ended up being a T.A. for him three years later.

Braces held more than my teeth back. I counted down the days I'd get them off, starting with the first afternoon they were installed. 730 days became 1,105 of them. I hated each of those one-thousand, one-hundred and five days. Before I got braces – back in 7th Grade – I loved my body. My muscles had popped before most other boys. Then the metal on my teeth came and I hated my body again. Then when the braces came off at the start of high school, acne flared all over my body. My hormones were exploding, but so were my pores. I couldn't get a girl to go out with me.

Cat snuck back in my life a full year after we met that day in Rosvik's class. We were in another class together Sophomore year. We kept bumping into each other. Social circles closed in. Halls got smaller. Lockers got closer. At a certain point there was no avoiding it. Eventually we went on a date, but it was contrived and I froze. We sat through an entire playhouse show and didn't say a word. Another year passed. Something pushed us apart. Then it pulled us back together again.

It was our Senior year when we fell in love, and we fell hard. There was no hope of not being in love with Wolf. That also was the very last time before anyone started getting infected.

That summer after our Senior year, we were supposed to be fretting about going off to college. We were supposed to be terrified of losing each other, of growing apart, living in different states, meeting new friends, finding our intellectual inspiration and, god save us, meeting someone else who might make us feel the same way we felt when we were together.

This was <u>not</u> the summer that we had. Instead it was the summer that the metal took hold.

After graduation, I got a laptop as a graduation present. I used it to chat with Wolf, write a bit, and play video games. The silicone and solder were just too effective at filling the voids between us. I thought that stupid computer was so awesome. Then it turned inside out and the parts starting growing everywhere. And I was part of the problem.

2

Wolf's Tale

Cat will tell you that we met in an unmemorable encounter in Mr. Rosvik's class. But I had my eyes on him for a long time before that. I wasn't necessarily attracted to him. He wasn't, like, the tallest, smartest or cutest boy in school. Come to think of it, I don't even know what I found interesting about him. I wasn't really aware of his talents (that's what lured me later). I had a pack of friends. The last thing I needed was another friend. It was just something about the way he held himself. It was like he never belonged where he was. He belonged *anywhere* he was. He fit in nowhere and everywhere. That was the attraction. You just wanted to be near him, whether you were aware of it or not. Cat had that effect on you.

I had to work to make myself fit in. I never quite passed with the cool kids. I leered around the fringes of coolness. I wasn't uncool enough for the nerdy clique. They all thought I was a priss. I had interesting gadgets, cool clothes and cute hair. I was too smart for popular packs, too pretty for unpopular packs. In many ways, Cat and I were both nowhere and everywhere at the same time.

Before Kate said, "Wolf, this is Cat," it wasn't my libido that was captured. A mysterious cat had caught my mind.

When Kate introduced us my mind went, *"ohhhhh, so THAT's why I can't let you go. You're a cat!"* And when our hands shook, they reverberated. Cat doesn't remember this. He will now.

We fell in love during our Senior year. We really fell in love — the terrifying, enrapturing kind — right before summer break at the end of that Senior year. It was right when all of us were trying to figure out what we were going to do with the rest of our lives. It was also the last time before it happened.

I was supposed to be going away to college. Cat and I were supposed to be scared of never seeing each other again. We were supposed to be the cliche teenage couple who's last summer fling becomes a sappy coming-of-age story dripping with the bittersweet nectar of life.

Hormones were supposed to be ravaging my body. The circumstances of my life were supposed to be out of my control. I was supposed to be blaming my parents for all of it.

Instead, all of the above was true, and more. We just had no idea how truly extreme it would all be. It's funny how extreme things make you forget so many other small details.

I remember my Dad's first mechanical tumor. I didn't blame him for it. It horrified me.

My first thought was, "How will this affect me?"

My second thought: "Will this affect whether I can see Cat or not?"

I can't say I feel for you if you've never been in love. I mean the ugly, nasty kind of love affair where you can't think straight, not for a single minute, not when you're apart, not when you're together. I'm almost envious if you've never felt this way about another person. Not everyone has. Some people stay married to the same person their entire lives without ever feeling something like this. They might get all mixed up in daily arguments and fleeting flashes of joy over their kid's achievements or a professional success. But getting hot and bothered in a marital tiff is different from being flush with obsessive thoughts about a person you love. Especially when you're apart from them.

I couldn't stop thinking about Cat when we were away from each other. I'd be in some other class at school or some other friend's house after school and think about him. I'd be in the car nowhere near seeing him and think of him. I'd be sitting with my family for dinner with no plans to see Cat and not be able to take a bite of food without thinking about him. Every song made me think of him. Every book and story. Every other person made me think of him. I see now that I was projecting the entire world onto him. But, man, it was fun. And maybe that's just what love is: mad obsessive projections.

Few would ever say that being madly in love is a clinically healthy thing to do, from a psychological perspective. But I'm not speaking from a clinical perspective here. I'm speaking from the perspective of a young woman who's travelled back in time 400 years to change things for all time to come. And Cat and I's love affair has everything to do with it.

Cat and I were forced apart right when we fell madly in love. We weren't forced apart by our parents, college plans, or our maturing minds. Robot cancer destroyed us. Sure, some parts of us came back. But some of the sweetest parts will never return.

3

Cat's Bite

I remember the first mechanical tumor I saw too. It was on my bus driver's wrist. I saw two thin hoses creeping out from the cuff of his sleeve. Out of respect, you never want to draw attention to someone's abnormality. Asking a disabled person how they became handicapped is like asking an obese lady if she's pregnant. You don't ask a Black person how they became Black. You don't ask a gay person how they became gay. You might ask how they announced it to the world. Even then - it should be with someone who trusts you.

All I could muster when I hopped off was, "Thank you." There must be thousands who step off public buses every day and rarely offer gratitude for the ride.

The nice, mechanically inclined driver replied, "You're welcome. Have a nice day."

I thought, *"Have a nice day? He has to be kidding. With a circuit board growing in your arm without your consent?"*

It's only the benefit of hindsight looking back on these things now. People weren't even bothered by them at first. When talking about a bit of machinery burrowing its way into some part of their body, some even thought, *"I'm a better person because of it."*

"Well, I can text and email a lot easier now, that's for sure," they'd say.

"Now I can check the weather and sports without even barely thinking about it!" They'd exclaim.

"I'm a freakin genius. Ask me anything! Ask me the square root of 983! Go ahead, ask me," an infected techno-zealot would say.

They had nary a thought for unwillingly giving it to other people around them. And <u>that</u>, my friends, is how they ran rough shot over the planet.

It was also highly under-reported at the time that the more technological devices were used, the more the viral disease would feed, fester and flourish. No, the evil super villain wasn't even the disease.

I remember the first time I caught a growth in my own arm too. I wasn't happy about it.

It wasn't long after the first wave of closures. I remember it well, because Wolf and I were so focused on each other and what we were missing. We couldn't get over it. It was all grief, all the time. Everything was shutting down. Even though theaters, restaurants and stadiums were all shuttering, we were convinced that it was just an elaborate rouse choreographed by our parents to keep us apart our families were two different heritages. It was easy being wrapped up in the adolescent hoax mind. But, before Wolf realized it too, I realized that we weren't just modern-day star crossed lovers.

I saw it growing in my arm. I'd just stepped out of the shower when I caught a glance in the mirror.

"That's weird." I ran my hand down my left arm. A thin sheet of metal was smoothing itself between my arm hair. It was the size of a narrow pencil, just slender and beneath enough skin to grow unnoticed for a day or so. It was hard to feel by touch. A rush of horror blew through me, "This is it. I'm a goner." I couldn't look at it. I turned from the mirror, collapsed and cried on the bathroom floor.

Mom was busy getting ready for work. She had the news on really loud, "…And that makes almost a half million reported infections to date."

I couldn't bear my next thought, "I'll never see her again." So I chomped down. There was a gush like watermelon. I didn't know what I was doing. I definitely wasn't intending to remove metal from my arm. But, as I had my mouth over it, I could feel it hum and whir. It beeped twice. That's when I chomped down harder.

Gouged inside the flesh of my arm, I closed and clenched until I felt them touch. Then I pulled. The metal ripped out. I spit it all in the toilet. I flushed, ferociously cleaned the bathroom, wrapped my arm, threw on a long sleeve shirt and ran out to work.

It was when I got to the job site that I knew something was way more wrong than my gouged arm. The foreman wouldn't get out of his car. Joe was a brawny mountain man. He was no new age boss who'd give single damn about work place progress or public health. He was a kind and decent man, but fully a product of bygone times when wealthy men ran the show without complaint. He was a typical old guy from a typical old part of America that's crossed by dusty old trains and people flying over it more often than remembering it. It was straight up spooky that my boss Joe would be spooked by anything. It was like he'd seen a ghost.

"Site's closed for the day," Joe said tersely from inside his locked truck. He wouldn't even roll down his window to talk to us. "You're all off for the week. We'll text you when it's ok to come back to work."

He knew something that I didn't. *What would it take for an old gruff like Joe to get so spooked?* There were enough alarm bells ringing in my ears already. Joe's rolled up window and locked door sent me reeling.

A text from Joe never came.

4

Wolf's Itch

Suddenly Mom and Dad wouldn't let me leave.

I was getting worked up, "You gotta be kidding me. Because of what they're saying in the news? That's why I can't see him?!"

Mom lowered her tone, "Honey, it's not us. I think our neighbor just turned into a blender."

I pleaded, "This is nuts. Dad?"

He wouldn't look at me. "Yeah, honey?" He was in open doorway of my room, alternating long stares between the ceiling and floor.

I asked, "What are you thinking?"

Dad scratched, picked and shared more gazes with the least picturesque parts of my room. "Not a lot. I just have this weird growth on my neck. Starting to worry me a little…"

Mom told me it'd only be a couple weeks. I believe her exact words were: "Two at the most. Look, we know you guys are being safe. And this isn't about you having sex."

"Mom!" I screamed in embarrassment.

Dad perked up, "Wait, since when were we talking about sex? You two aren't having sex, are you?"

"GREAT. Thanks, Mom. Can you two get out of here now? I'd like to start my isolation now." They retreated from my door and closed it behind them.

An argument flared in the hall as they walked away, "What do you mean: *I should have it looked at*? YOU DON'T THINK I'M BEING CAREFUL??"

My mind wouldn't stop spinning that night, the next morning, the next day, next night, next morning and on. I couldn't get over it. I couldn't get past anything. Everything bore down. The weight of the entire world fit squarely inside the love between Cat and I. We couldn't satiate it with calls and texts.

At 3 a.m. we were video chatting and it wasn't going well. I was getting moody, "I just can't think about anything else. I hate it. It's like I've lost total control of everything I'm feeling. I hate my parents. I hate my life. I hate myself for not being in control of myself." I was under the covers to muffle the sound and light from my laptop. Cat could still see me crying. "And we have no idea when this will be over."

"Maybe our parents are just freaking out," Cat said.

"I can't even tell that any more. Every time I try to read news or my feed, everything points in every direction. Maybe it's all a hoax. Maybe everyone is making this up in their mind. Maybe it's totally for real and we really are under attack. Maybe this is the end. Who knows!"

He asked, "What does your heart tell you?"

I answered, "That I love you."

Cat started to cry. He was huddled under his blankets too. Fortunately our parents were heavy sleepers and weren't savvy enough to check the data rates in the middle of the night. We were burning it up.

"I dream of a day when we can just spend the night together. When we don't have to have this damn screen between us. When we can just be together, you know? No time limits, no separations. Nothing keeping us apart. Then we can just… be," Cat wept.

"I know, baby. I know exactly what you mean," I consoled.

"I love you so much, Wolfie. It's killing me. I have to see you," he said.

"I want you inside me again," I said.

Cat sighed, "Oy. You're killin me baby."

I was exasperated, "We're not supposed to go out."

"Just once."

"But the virus…"

"I've been safe. You've been safe. It won't hurt anything if we just meet once."

"Can you sneak out?" I asked.

"I think so," Cat guessed, "same place?"

"Same place."

5

Cat's Prowl

Our houses are on the far ends of town. Wolf and I live on the opposite end of the tracks, just not in that cliche kind of way. We both come from the modest means that land most folks in a shabby middle America nowheresville like ours. There's been enough exposure for this town to be slightly woke, just enough not to start a race riot over families like ours settling, at least. It's predominantly a white place but for it's lack of ethnic diversity, all of us - not just, angsty teenage young ones - in this crappy little town share the common bonds of wanting to get out of it; to rise above our means.

My Dad's Dad immigrated from Nigeria. Dad left when I was young. Mom supports me on her own.

Wolf's Mom grew up in a Korean deli her parents started soon after they arrived. She inherited it when they passed. Wolf's Dad came into the store, became a regular and they fell in love. Then he had a freak accident. He had a promising career working his way up middle management of a health care processing facility. But after the accident, he fell on hard times.

Unemployment and disability took a heavy toll. The bottle came into play.

So a little dusty deli on the edge of town is still the main source of income for Wolf's whole family. We're on opposite ends of the tracks, but we're on the same side of the railroad. And this railroad bisects a town so alike so many other towns in middle American. It makes me want to vomit. The boredom of this place makes me ill. Our town is truly the last place where you'd expect a revolution to happen.

Wold and I barely ended up at the same high school. I live far enough away that I could've enrolled in school at the next town over. There was a larger force at play when I decided to register where I did.

When we wanted to see each other outside school, Wolf and I would borrow a car or, on occasions when the timing was right, hop the train to each other's house. Our tracks didn't run passenger or commercial liners. Only rusty freighters came barreling down, usually at odd hours. The day time runs were less regular but there was always a 4 a.m. train going by.

Kids and hobos hopped trains in our town all the time. Everyone knew about the hobos. They didn't try very hard to hide and usually hopped off in our town for amenities before hopping back on. Wolf's family deli was one of their regular haunts and her Mom didn't mind. She was a generous person despite their lot. She'd let them use her bathroom to wash up. She even let them short her on a till, so long as they didn't shoplift. That hit a nerve stretching back well beyond her own neural network. Some traumas sting so hard that just won't leave a family's DNA.

What most parents in our town didn't know is that their kids were using the same jumping points as the hobos; that we were turning freight trains into commuter lines. We'd deliver lines like, "I'm getting a ride with Fred," or, "Ethel's giving me a ride." The 4 a.m. line was a particularly useful one for getting to or from someone's house late at night. I could come up with a story to convince my parents that I needed to stay late at school for sports or studying, get a ride with someone to Wolf's house, then go romp in the fields behind her house until the sky began to turn from black to dark blue. We'd break from making out just enough to catch the first light hitting the modest cluster of dilapidated, one-story buildings that composed our small town. Her Dad was glued to the TV. Her Mom was glued to the store. We could even rendezvous at the deli after Wolf was done helping, then run off after that. Long afternoons stretched through that spring of our Senior year, and into the summer.

I'd hop that 4 a.m. line home with a big, shit-eating grin plastered all over my face. I could still feel Wolf's skin on my mine for hours after we parted. It wasn't just memory. My fingers would tingle as if I was still touching her. My chest would vibrate like her hands were still on me. My lips would still quiver deep into the next day, 6-7 hours later after our last kiss. My body kept her alive in me for the passages of time that we were apart. And it worked really well, because it was usually just those 6, 7, maybe 8 hours that I needed to last before I'd see her again. We could always count on seeing each at school in the morning. The weekends were more of a challenge, but we could find plenty of real or fake activities to bring us back together on any given Saturday or Sunday. This is what that sticky, gooey kind of being-in-love is: counting down the hours and minutes apart. What we never anticipated was counting down centuries and eons.

Later that night, and into the following morning after I chewed the metal out of my arm, after we were pushed to the brink on our video chat, Wolf hopped the 4 a.m. towards my place. I heard it coming.

We'd gotten good enough at jumping on and off to remove most of the risk involved. The train slowed as it passed through the short, 1-mile section of our town. We never saw it going faster than 15 mph. The riskier part was trying to hop the exact same train as someone else. If you hopped the same train on different cars, you had to climb up on top. The freight cars didn't have doors, ramps and passages between them. They were designed for cargo.

I got out of the house and timed it just right. I hopped on as it rolled by, just beyond our backyard. At that moment, as I climbed to the top of the train car I'd hopped, I didn't know if Wolf was actually on the train.

Uneasily standing on the roof of the rumbling car, I looked up and down the train. I could see the engine but not the caboose. Wolf wasn't up front. She wasn't on any of the roofs. I started toward the back, "She must be back there somewhere. At least if I head this way, she won't double back and pop up somewhere towards the front."

The last cars came into view. I started to worry, "Ugh! I'm headed to our spot without her!"

She popped up a ladder right in front of me. "Hi!" Our lips wrapped together before I could return a verbal greeting. Our arms melded with no space for air between us. The kiss lasted ten minutes. Neither of us wanted to stop. Blood flowed towards groins. It got real hot, even up there on top of a moving train in a cool evening breeze.

Our lips finally parted enough to choose words. Wolf squeezed her arms tighter and closed her eyes. "Mmm, I *missed* you." We walked hand in hand towards the back. Rear cars were a good place to jump. We had a field to get to.

"Why does a few hours feel like days?" Wolf asked as we climbed another car.

I was hurrying, "I don't know, babe. But we gotta pick up the pace. We're gonna miss our spot."

Still holding hands, we separated slightly, at arm's length, just to give ourselves room to run.

The rumbling cars picked up their pace. We felt a lurch as the engineer accelerated. The train passed Ted's Auto Body Shop, Hal's Saloon and Fran's Barber Shop. We passed the second and last gas station. We were at edge of town.

We sped up, running faster and faster. Cars moved faster under our feet.

That is when, and I can't describe this and clearer: the ground under us paused. Only the train moved. We were running in place.

Tons of steel flowed under our feet. We flashed giant goofy grins at each other while we ran. Faster and faster we picked up the pace.

"IT FEELS LIKE WE'RE NOT GOING TO GET TO THE END," I huffed and puffed in stride.

"I KNOW! LIKE WE AREN'T GETTING ANYWHERE!" Wolf shouted back. But we were getting somewhere. We were rapidly approaching the end of the train as the train approached the end of our town that approaches so quick, you'll miss it if you wink. Running hand in hand, we hit top speed just before getting to the end of the last car.

That is when it happened. That's the last I saw of Wolf.

My heart was pounding for her. My groin was aching for her. My soul was expanding for her.

Then, POOF. She was gone. Everything was gone.

I was immediately traveling in a straight line up and away without her.

6

Wolf's Jump

I love him, but I have a tendency to question Cat's memory. In this case, he has the facts straight. It happened just like that. We were teenagers in love running over a midnight train on a hot summer night. Then we weren't. Cat vanished from my hand as fast as my heart raced for him.

I was still on top of that train. Or at least, I thought I was. I had no idea I was on a different train entirely. Train technology hasn't advanced much in a couple hundred years. It took me a while to figure out that I'd been transported to another century.

It happened right when Cat and I hit that point when it seemed like the ground stopped moving under us. We were running together at the same exact speed as the train, but in the opposite direction that it was traveling. So when we looked down at the ground, we could see every part of it, the rocks, dirt and grass. We really *had* stopped moving on a moving train. Then it all went haywire.

"He was sitting on a train when it hit. Eureka! Epiphany happened," I remembered Mr. Mintech lecturing in Physics. "The genius had been trying to figure out how it all strung together. The train made him see the thing that stitched the whole universe into one cohesive quilt."

I tried recalling more, "What was it that Mintech said after? That's right: *everything is relative*. Time is relative. It moves differently depending on where you are. Years on Earth are different from years on Mars, and Mars' rotation around the sun is different from Earth's. But then there are other suns in other solar systems out there."

More memories came, "Years can pass in a totally different way than in our solar system. Planets closest to a sun in another solar system could be all spread out. The years on another planet could pass at an agonizingly slow pace. Planets in another solar system could be bunched together close to the sun, with years sailing by like days."

I wondered, "So would inhabitants of planets like this age really quickly? Would their bodies decay quicker? Or would the number assigned to their age just advance faster as their bodies decay the same as humans?"

I remember Mintech crescendo-ing with a wry declaration, "It's all relative."

Somewhere in my memories was the answer to what happened to Cat and I on top of that train. Cat disappeared, and I was on top of another train. I just had no idea when or where. I always loved Mintech's class. It was bringing me comfort. It just wasn't delivering answers.

The train cars under my feet had changed dramatically. They were black, covered in soot and rickety as all get out. The tracks weren't flat or straight. The freight cars that Cat and I jumped would rumble over tracks with a certain wobble, but nothing like this. I could barely stand. It had way less flat area on top. The edges of the roof curved over the tops of the walls. The steel wasn't the manufactured and factory painted brick-red variety that rolled by the backyards and dirty windows of our shabby houses. The steel used to assemble these train cars wasn't manufactured. It was beaten to shape by hand. I was on top of an antique.

I climbed over the back edge. There were passengers inside. They didn't see me at first. A window peered through the back door of the car's platform I stood on. It was caked in dirt and grime. I ducked low to gather my wits.

My mind turned, "Why are there passengers riding the freight train? How did the cars turn old? Why are they all Black? Where the *HELL* is my Kitty Cat?"

I slowly stood up. There they were, a full train car full of passengers sitting in rows. All were facing front with their hands in their laps. We rolled a bump in the tracks and I hit the back window. THUD. I ducked down again. Someone turned to look back. I snuck up to again. All of them faced forward again.

The few other minority families in our town and neighboring counties were not enough to fill a train car. Cat and I usually stood out, even though we were both only half. Our families were generally treated with respect. The worst was when, because of our slightly darker complexions, people would try – even with good intention – identifying our ethnicity. *"Are you from Mexico?"*

"I don't know, I can't place it. You look like a Hawaiian I once knew."

"Are you part Native American?"

And so on. It always came from the same place. Cat and I were lucky to escape any physical harm. We weren't targeted by malice. We just suffered the same dull, persistent churn of the under-the-skin infections that won't leave this world alone. Or at least, not the world as we know it.

If the sickness had left us alone a long time ago, it sure as hell would have made us all a lot less susceptible to the infections, that's for damn sure.

It was around that same day, early after the infections started to really spread, that they started the first desperate attempts at a treatment – not a cure or immunization, just a slap-dash quick fix. Amputation was it. They also removed peoples' teeth at first, because many of the infections originated and festered in the mouth. They especially enjoyed breeding from existing metal in the human body. Cavity fillings were some of the most common metal bits in our bodies, so that's where a lot of infections started. But cutting out limbs and molars was like modern-day chemotherapy: dark age medical treatment with a short sighted fate. They amputated limbs and emptied mouths of teeth that would never return. Throngs were voluntarily disabled for no good reason.

I was standing there, disturbed by the unfamiliarities stacking higher and higher. Someone in the car mouthed, "Look! A girl!" Others turned to look, but they didn't get up. They couldn't. They were all chained together. Their hands were bound to each other, and to the bench seats they sat in.

7

Cat's Leap

Wolf disappeared from my hand but nothing else disappeared from my view. I was still on top of the freight container. It's just that, and I don't really know how else to explain this, the car and I were floating in the air. The cargo container and I had disconnected and lifted directly off the train. We were ascending directly upwards from the point on the tracks when Wolf left me. The rest of the train kept rolling on. I was way up in the air.

I slowly knelt down to crawl and look over the edge of the container roof. I must have been several thousand feet in the air and climbing steadily. There was nothing under the cargo container, nothing above it. Unless a tiny little Superman was under there flying me upward, I had no explanation for how I was flying on a train car. All I knew is that it was starting to get cold.

"If we keep getting higher, the air's gonna get real thin," I thought. "Might be time to try getting inside this thing."

The doors of a modern cargo container are impossible to open from on top, even when it's not floating in mid air. Two latches are designed to unlatch from below. Just getting down to the latches from above, with no ground to catch my fall, was tricky. I had to hoist myself down, using the door's vertical latching bars, then hang like Spiderman, swinging my legs up and below the container. S'pose I should say, being an actual Black Cat and all, that I was a real Black Panther handling myself up there. And just as I'm writing this, I'm realizing now what a bad luck omen I've always been. I've capitalized my own Black Cat so much that I never even thought of it in the lower case.

Anyway, it took real jostling to open those latches without the ground to push against. Those doors must have weighed a few hundred pounds each. "Rusty! Of course that's my luck."

I unlocked latches to force one door open. I pried it enough to slip my upper body through. BOOM. The door's weight swung back and clamped my waist. "That's gonna bruise." My hips radiated as I pushed to shimmy my legs inside. Once in, the door THUD shut. I latched it closed from the inside.

It was full of cardboard boxes. Almost all were marked from Amazon. "Well, this *is* my luck. A good thing, for once. Because I might be stuck in here a while."

The container shuttered. It wasn't the hard rumble of tracks. The container walls wobbled and bounced. POP! Two plates indented inward. From working in the yards for Joe and a life living on the tracks, I'd seen cargo containers stacked, packed and re-used all kinds of ways. I was well acquainted with steel work. Joe had worked in the mill so when he opened his yard, he brought his experience with him, and to me. Still, I couldn't imagine how a steel cargo container could collapse inward under pressure, "Even changes in the Earth's atmosphere wouldn't do it." Safely - I thought – locked inside a flying cargo container, it was time for a look outside.

Modern day cargo containers go through a lot of pre-fab. Tons are made in China on the fly. Joe says they're taking away our jobs. Maybe he's right. I just know that if I were in the yard welding away on the walls of cargo containers all day, I'd do it a lot better than they do nowadays.

The plates of the walls and ceiling were deeply dented, but they had no holes. The doors were well sealed. The welds at the corners of the walls, ceiling and floor were holding. "Hmm. I'm impressed. Maybe the robots are getting right," I surmised.

There was a rectangular patch on the wall where a sign was hung. Dust and soot hadn't collected. The dust-free patch was high on the wall above several boxes. I moved some boxes for a better look. One of the holes where the sign was bolted had been patched with a quick weld.

The other sign-handing hole went through the container's ribbing. Some dunce had hung the sign. I can't tell you how the sign read. It was long gone. But I can tell you exactly how the installation of that sign read. It read, "Watch out. Idiot at work." The fool had drilled through both sheets of steel that sandwich together to make the container's double-walls. The hole pierced the two steel plies that separate into a hollow column - one of the hollow columns that, as I understood and trusted from my experience, gave the container its strength.

I climbed over a box to press my eye and squint into the column's overly drilled screw hole. It never got plugged. At first when I looked through, it all looked black, "Hmm. Must be plugged from the outside." I remembered it was still pretty dark out. We'd caught the 4 a.m. train. Sunrise wasn't for another hour.

I rotated my head in different angles to switch my trajectories looking through the unfilled screw hole. I caught a glimpse outside. The container walls shimmered again. Another steel plate popped with a BOOM. The whole container resonated.

It was dark outside but not just because of the Earth's rotation around the sun. That was, in fact, becoming less relevant by the minute.

BOOM. Another plate popped.

The air didn't feel as thin as it did when I was out on top of the container, after I sailed away from the tracks. Looking through the screw hole, I saw strange refractions from inside the wall's hollow steel column. The hollow column had somehow been filled with epoxy or glass.

Stars were getting brighter. The ground was getting a lot further away. I could barely make details below. And at a certain angle, an enormous curvature took hold. It shook me to my core. I'm telling you: I was in space.

8

Wolf's Trap

I could feel Cat. I could feel him close. I could also feel that he was far way. My skin still vibrated from his touch but there I was, some little kid on the back of some old ass train full of chained slaves. And they were bearing down on me.

The commotion of seeing me settled. Most of them returned to face front, but they were up to something. Their heads moved a lot. Before they saw see me, their heads faced front and down, like they were sleeping, and I woke them up. They were talking to each other. A plan was hatching. Words passed between seats and worked back to my dusty window.

I cowered and considered jumping. I'd jumped plenty of trains in my life. This one was only going a little faster and there was soft ground I could land on. I could've easily bolted at that moment.

Something held me in place.

We'd been dating a few months. I'd never considered leaving Wolf, but we all know stories about lovers leaving each other. Instead I wondered about those who stuck together. Because I couldn't imagine anything ever making me want to leave Wolf. I thought about what it was that keeps people together. "What is it - when times get hard, when things get messy - that keeps people from leaving each other?" I wondered. I thought about a lover who doesn't leave their spouse who becomes disabled, or cheats on them. I thought about people who don't shy away from the people they love when they're going through tough times.

Then I noticed it inside me, cowering on the back of that train car full of enslaved people, "This must be what makes lovers want to leave each other." It must have been coursing inside of me. The same feeling must have been what was holding me there in place.

The plan arrived. KNOCK KNOCK went the door from the inside. I stood up. The two sitting closest to the window beckoned me. One put her finger to her lips to sign, "Shhh."

The other moved his mouth in really big motions so I could read his lips through the old window, "*The guard stands in front. Do not make a sound.*"

I nodded.

"*You can open this door from out there.*" The man pointed, "*Wobble that latch.*"

It squeaked like a fat mouse. Everyone inside cringed. Shoulders hunched and heads bowed. Everyone but the two talking with me looked forward. They all froze.

The woman exclaimed without a sound, "DUCK DOWN!"

I ducked out of view, but peaked through a tiny dirt clearing in the bottom corner of the window. The guard opened the front of the train and stepped in. He passed each row of bench seats and inspected everyone's hands. He was a middle-aged white man with a hat full of holes. It looked like he hadn't bathed in weeks.

"EYES FORWARD," he bellowed as he clubbed one man on the side of the head. He kept walking towards the back. When he got to the last rows, I receded from the window corner. I tucked in the front corner of the caboose's platform. Being small became beneficial.

I could hear dust shuffle between his soles and the floor. Dirt, pebbles and grains of sand kicked out from each step. My heart pounded. The sounds deafened. I sensed danger with every fiber of my being.

In school we were taught about Harriet Tubman, the underground railroad, Rosa Parks, and Dr. King. I'd never heard of an over-ground railroad of slaves. We'd been taught about how Africans were shipped overseas under abhorrent conditions on slave ships. It wasn't a big leap to imagine similar conditions on rails.

I knew about southern plantations, the slave labor that built so much of our country's infrastructure, and how it all related to the Civil War.

Cat wept hard when we watched "Roots". His Dad left him too young to bring him a sense of place and heritage he had to get from books and movies.

He wound up growing up identifying with Michael Jordan, Bill Cosby and Jackson as father figures.

Alex Haley, Levar Burton, Alice Walker and Toni Morrison painted exacting pictures. Still, even the best books and movies can never give you that intangible feeling of what it's like to be there. Even the grittiest, most honest depictions of the most horrible conditions humans have ever suffered can't strike the fear into your heart like actually being there.

There I was, about to be caught by a slave master. I was a half-Asian girl about to feel what's it like to be a real slave. Cat desperately wanted to connect with his African-American history. I was about to connect with it for him.

The guard leaned into the window from inside the car and pressed his face to the glass. The train hit another huge bump in the tracks. BAM! The side of his head slammed against the glass. Some snickered.

"SHUT UP! EYES FRONT!!" He yelled and bashed the shoulders of the two who were talking me. The train hit another bump. "SQUEEK!" Went the door. The guard wheeled around. The train bumped again and again, another, "SQUEEK!" He watched the door. I kept pressed into the corner outside. Another BUMP and SQUEEK happened.

"Damn old trains," he muttered and started walking back to the front. My shoulders relaxed with each step he took.

What little education I'd had about the history of slavery was enough to send shutters through all parts of me. Maybe teachers and history books glossed over gory details for good reason. Maybe young minds couldn't handle hearing about the actual conditions. This was becoming clearer to me the more my body shuttered with fear. As much as I could understand, and as little as I had been taught, the palpable sense of terror was more intense than anything I'd ever felt. Even my most intense moments of love with Cat couldn't match it.

I sat there on the back of that train for a moment, waiting for my skin to stop crawling, for the goosebumps to settle, for the guard to keep walking off.

I sat there realizing what that one moment of fear felt like. I had only been there a few minutes. The people inside the train had been there who knows how long. "And who knows how many people have felt this way for how long?"

I wondered, "*What would Cat do?*" Then I knew.

9
Cat's Cage

The panic of being stuck in a box mixed with the wonder of floating in space. It was hard to sort the two emotions apart from each other. I would've lost it if it weren't for my little peep hole.

Not knowing where you, or for how long you'll be there, will drive a person insane when they're stuck in captivity. It's amazing what a little bit of information and context will do for someone who's trapped. Even long-time convicts know their own sentence, when their next parole hearing will be, or what state their prison is located in. It's the uncertainty that's most deeply woven into the fear of being marooned on a desert island. You might get sick of eating the same fruits and swimming in the same warm water of a tropical paradise. But if you happen to fall in love with the place that's confining you, you still don't know how long the good thing will last. Settle in and prepare for the long haul, or prepare for a rescue? Are we all inhabiting a captivity of our own making?

Never mind not knowing where I was, or how long I'd be there. At least I could see what planet she was on. Otherwise my thoughts of Wolf alone would have been rattling around inside that container way too violently.

My cargo container was rising at a steady clip. Surface details were gone. Cloud formations obscured land and water. Water, water, water. What fools we are to price the land we covet so highly. There we are, tiny little humans, crowded onto little tufts of dry Earth, surrounded on all sides by a substance we'd die both without, and constantly destroy. The perspective of our pale blue dot was nothing if not sobering.

Stacks of Amazon boxes stared back at me. Only bits of the rough wood planks bolted the container floor's steel frame were visible. Most of the boxes were strapped on pallets when they were hoisted in. More loose boxes were stacked on top of the crated ones.

The ceiling was eight feet tall inside. I could stretch my arms and touch. Boxes were stacked just above eye level. There were a few slots between them where I could see container walls, and get to my peep hole. Claustrophobia would've been an issue if I was totally boxed in. Nonetheless, it was time to open things up.

While tearing into the first box, I imagined my defense on trial, *"Several laws of gravity and physics had already been broken. If the laws of physics didn't apply anymore, I didn't know what rules would apply any more. Opening the mail should have been the least of anyone's concerns."*

Office supplies were in the first rows. They must've been shipments bound for small businesses. Somebody ordered blocks of Post-It notes, adhesive folder labels, and college-ruled paper. "This stuff could be interesting." They'd also filled their shopping cart with plenty of office snacks. It looked like breakfast would be composed from the cartridges of some trendy "BreakfastBot" gadget somebody bought to impress someone else at the office. Lunch would be served from buckets of preservative-laden peanut butter pretzels and medium-stale Red Vines. Dinner would be Hot Tamales, the high fructose and maltodextrin variety.

Wolf and I would meet for lunch at the taco truck run by another family who posted on the street outside her family's deli. Their specialty was fresh tamales. They made their own salsa and mole. They wrapped and cooked the masa to perfection. The tamales were never too moist, never too dry. All their different fillings — spicy chicken, pulled beef or rice and beans — were spot on.

Holding a giant box of "hot tamales" while floating in space in a cargo container, anticipating the savory concoction that my new house-pet-sized BreakfastBot might serve, I started missing reality terribly. I hated my meal options. I missed Wolf like hell. The tears were hard to fight.

Of course, my FOMO failed to reconcile with what I was actually missing back down on Earth. In the few short weeks after the first cases were reported, it'd ripped across vast geographic areas. The highly infectious cancer's virological development was greatly aided by peoples' casual, nonchalant acceptance of personal responsibility for public health safety. People weren't just callously and wantonly spreading a disease. They weren't just dying painful, inglorious deaths because of it. In the fatal course of the cancer, the bodies of innocently infected people grew bells, whistles, servos, gears, and belts while transforming into editing reels, portable generators, bullhorns, air compressors, AC/DC converters, gas pumps, Amazon drop boxes, ATM machines, transformer boxes, X-ray machines, CT scanners and sewage pumps. Slap dash treatments were being used to amputate limbs. Experimental organ transplants were being used to swap out electric pencil sharpeners, motorized can openers and robotic infant toys that had grown in place of lungs, kidneys, hands and feet.

For those who were staying home and thwarting the spread of the disease, they were also fostering its growth. They were buying new air hockey tables, lap tops and talking dolls to satiate the boredom of being stuck in the house. And so the disease fed on boredom too, slowly creeping up a leg, crawling over the hips, under the arm and down the wrist with its tiny transistors and transmitters. Brand new Sonos speakers, rice makers, waffle irons and water coolers were appearing out of thin air in the kitchens, living rooms and offices of everyone on Earth.

My location over Earth shifted west. "If this keeps up, I'll be orbiting in the opposite direction." Something about this was comforting, "I might rotate back. I might see her again."

I feverishly rummaged the office supply boxes. "Where are those damn post-it notes?!?" Unpacked things were strewn, but I didn't want to unpack too much. I didn't know how long I'd be stuck there. I definitely didn't want to settle in and unpack everything. But the thought did occur to me, "I might have to settle in at some point." That was decidedly <u>un</u>settling.

I'd checked my phone on the way up. The battery was already low before I left. There wasn't much of a signal once the container started floating, only enough to update the clock. It just gave me a good idea for what time it was when I left. I had a starting point. I knew the time and place of where and when I left. From that point, I just needed to start making my own reference points.

"The phone will also ping my location," I thought. "Even if it only pings two or three more times, that'll be plenty for them to start tracking my trajectory and come find me. But they'd have to launch a whole new space mission just to save me, or re-route someone else already in space. All of that could take a while. I better use those pings for my own reference too. I gotta write all this down."

I thought I'd get saved but I didn't know when. "No one has time to go find some Black teenager in space. Even if they launched a shuttle mission tomorrow, or sent an envoy straight from the nearest space station, it'd take weeks. The infections are nowhere near letting up. They're not even close to a cure. I could be here for years."

Degrees of uncertainty like this send different people in different directions at different times. I could've lost it right then, bounced off the walls, chewed off my arm, or strung myself up with a new laptop charging cord freshly unpacked from Amazon. I didn't have the benefits of a Buddhist to enjoy my solitude and unique opportunity to reach Zen. How was I supposed to enjoy this? Or make the most of it? First, I was forced to separate from Wolf. Those last couple weeks before I left were hell, to be held back from seeing her like that. That was enough of a prison. Now this.

We all adjust to extreme circumstances differently, sometimes even at different times of the day. I might cope with the same circumstance one way one part of the day, then cope with the exact same circumstance differently later on the same day. Hope, despair and everything in between were all in the tool box to adapt to the isolation and uncertainty I was facing.

Pulling one of the more unexpected tools from the box, I was fighting an instinct to nest. Images of the container and its contents neatly organized rushed through my mind. I imagined a row of boxes covered into a bed, others made into chairs and a table, the rest working as shelves. One corner would be my kitchen and bath. One corner would be a work space. A sleeping nook could be made with a makeshift wall of boxes creating a cozy partition. All this was appearing very clearly in my mind's eye. All of it had to be swept away.

The unpacked boxes were not inviting me. I should've felt like I'd landed a sweet haul on Storage Wars. Instead they were just intimidating me. Some made noise, hummed, beeped, whirred and chirped.

"Well, that might explain the anti gravity and oxygen being emitted."

I scrambled into one of the boxes of unpacked office crap. "Gotta find those post-it notes. Yes!" I uncapped a fresh Sharpie from an unopened 10-pack. I checked my peephole again. I was moving fast. I had to keep track. I had to reach outward or inward. Considering my predicament, I had only one choice.

Mom said that my Dad was a cool cat, sometimes too cool. She said it was hard to get him to care about things. He'd act like he was off on some other planet, lost in his own thoughts. That must have been nice. What I wouldn't have given for that luxury, but my reality was too close. All I wanted was to be dragged back down to Earth.

Dad left Mom when she was pregnant with me. He came back briefly when I was about 2, then left again for good when I was 3. I don't have memories of him. Apparently he was articulate and well educated. This never jived. How could such a smart person give up on such a huge responsibility? If you're such an educated man, what brilliant line of thinking leads you to the conviction that you need to leave your only child? What bothered me the most was that Mom would defend him.

"He just had to live his own life," she'd say. *"You wouldn't have wanted him around if he didn't want to be here. It just wouldn't have worked."*

I'd remind her of him. *"Your father was just like that."* She'd pause a moment then say something like, *"He was a great man."* This would piss me off. I didn't want to upset Mom, so I'd just get really quiet and bottle it all up.

This of course, would remind her of him too.

"*Gone quiet again, hmm? Cat got your tongue, hmm? Just like your father… Stoic and aloof like the cat,*" she'd recite affectionately and condescendingly, "*my cool little kitty Cat.*"

When Dad left Mom alone with me growing inside, she said to me, "*I'm gonna name you Cat. Doesn't matter if you're a boy or girl. I'm taking it back.*"

The mantle was reclaimed, but I didn't want him inside me. I was too mad.

Yet there he was, crawling his way out, preening and pawing with sweet indifference to the world surrounding him. I didn't want to reclaim him. I also didn't want to be floating in a box above the Earth's atmosphere.

I had to do some real hunting to survive this one. No one was around to help me hunt and flush it out. No one was there to help me tackle it. This cat was on his own. I sure was one damned unlucky Black cat.

10

Wolf's Run

When my Mom was a kid in Korea, she was left alone to her own devices with her brothers and sisters. Grandma was busy handling a large family and Grandpa was always working. As a kid, Mom ended up taking care of a lot of stray dogs. She'd feed and clean them without bringing them in the house. The whole neighborhood appreciated it because strays weren't a nuisance like they were in other neighborhoods. Mom connected with them. She watched mothers take care of pups, unrelated dogs relate to each other in a pack, and survive by relying on one another. She was proud of them. Hers didn't fight for scraps like other strays. Fights in her packs were settled quickly. They learned to bring food (when they got it) to the young and most vulnerable. They learned to share.

Mom's parents immigrated, settled in the US, and her and Dad started the deli. When Mom was pregnant with me while working at the deli, a pack of wolves frequented the alley for trash in the morning and evening. She was inspired to do the same nurturing she gave her strays as a kid back in Korea.

She also knew better than to try taming wild animals. She didn't feed or try contacting with them. They'd sneak in the alley and rummage trash. She'd pull up a chair. Dad caught her sitting, sometimes a full hour, staring out the window at the alley wolves. Other neighbors were horrified. Fish & Wildlife was called but said they wouldn't do anything until the wolves harmed humans or other animals. So neighbors learned to sit and watch too, like Mom, with wonder.

One late night while watching the wolves, she held her belly engorged with me inside. *"I'm going to name you Wolf whether you're a boy or girl. You will be loved and love another, just like they do. You will take care of others and be well taken care of."*

As soon as the train guard was out of sight and ear shot, I resumed talking with the two through the back window, "I know how to jump trains."

"But you're just a girl."

I was a full-grown 18 year-old, but my half-Asian blood gave me a rather diminutive stature. I looked young for my age. And I was thrown into a tough period of time. Even young children were forced to grow up quick and learn things no child should ever be forced to learn. I didn't correct their assumption that I was a runaway. I just wanted them free.

"The latch down below," the woman gestured. "Grab and pull it up with your foot."

"Got it. Now what?"

"Now pull that upper latch at the same time."

"You're kidding, right? I can't reach that," I said.

"Just try. You can do it," she said.

I curled my toe under a rusty old door latch on the back of the 19th Century slave train car. I reached as far as I could to the top of the door. My limbs stretched like cheese on a hot slice of pizza. My left leg extended downward while my right arm reached up. I got the upper latch. My body was pulled tight across the back of that door, loosely bumping it like a taught sail slaps a mast. I was a rag doll hanging there thinking, "Just don't let go."

The two of them giggled, "Now pull!"

The train hit another bump in the tracks. BAM! With my grip still held tight, the bump shook the latches loose. It swiveled open with me still attached to the back, and gently landed against the back of the train. I de-clawed and got down to introduce myself.

It was the first time I saw chains around wrists and ankles. "This is gonna be harder than I thought." All of them were shackled.

"Little miss, you've already done so much for us," the woman said, "My name is Odonna. This is Harry. We'll introduce the rest soon, but now we gotta go."

I curtseyed, "Please to meet you. I'm Wolf." The rest of the car tried not to raise a commotion while gathering to run. Those in front kept an eye on the door for the guard. He and two other guards had three cars to watch. They'd rotated in and out of the car already. It was a good time.

I asked, "Are you shackled to each other, or the train?"

"We're in pairs, ma'am," Harry responded.

"We have some little ones, sick and elderly folk, but we're ready. We can jump," Odonna assured.

I told them, "This might be hard to believe, but I've probably jumped on and off trains thirty times in my life. You know about tucking your head and rolling?"

"Relay that down the line," Odonna motioned.

"And kicking out to land on your back?"

"Relay that too," Odonna motioned again.

"And be prepared for a hard tumble. Protect your head. Tuck your limbs in a ball. Think of yourself like a football," I said.

"A what?" Harry asked.

I realized, "No football yet…. Just get ready to roll!"

"Pass all that down the line now," Odonna said.

"And bring your shackles around the back of your neck. You don't want those chains bashing your face when you hit the ground," I said. Harry whispered my instructions down the line.

Odonna took a hard stare, "Miss Wolf, I don't know where you came from or how you got on the back of this train. And I don't know how you know all you know, being the young woman that you are. It's like someone or something sent you here to help us. I don't know if it's the same God who we pray to each and every day, but I thank God, now nonetheless, for you being here."

I admitted, "I don't really know how I got here either, Odonna. I just know I need all of us off this train. Now."

She flashed a mouth of happy teeth. "Well let's go then, child."

Back home people were being shackled with – albeit in a different form – metal chains of another variety. Even for the tech lovers of the world, a metamorphosis from human to machine was losing its romantic ring. No summer blockbuster would give it a Hollywood ending. The disease was blocking and busting the summer too much, as it was. People kept going out, congregating and passing it between one another with ease. They wanted to be in bondage. They'd given up life already, before the disease arrived. When it arrived, they were too far gone, "*I wasn't free in the first place, before the robot cancer. So why should I care to free myself from bondage now?*"

One particularly disease-spreading bit was that people thought they were immune if they'd been exposed but hadn't grown any electronics or machinery in their body. It could be months later. The metal, tubes, hoses and wires would always kick in. Belts and would grow in the arms and legs. Pumps and compression chambers would form in the abdomen. Eventually, every infected person would become entirely trapped in a machine.

Two by two, they jumped and tumbled off the train just like I said. The ground was a mix of loose soil and grass leading into pastures. I noticed the train travelled relatively slow. "The conductor must've slowed down with all those bumps in the tracks."

Odonna helped another pair jump off. "We've got good luck and timing on our side."

Harry hoisted two more off, "And a good Wolf on our side, too,"

Odonna said, "It's a blessing to have a hunter looking out for us."

I told them, "You've got a good pack assembled. This car will be empty before we know it." The last to jump were watching the front door. The guards were still busy in other cars. The watchers jumped. Odonna, Harry and I jumped last.

45 Black folks were on the ground stretching a half mile down the tracks. The young, sick and elderly composed themselves. 44 of us were still in shackles. The train rolled on.

Odonna yelled down the line, "KEEP YOUR HEADS DOWN. WE DON'T WANT THEM TO CATCH AN EYE DOWN THE TRACK AND STOP THE TRAIN." We crawled and slid down the slope off the tracks. It would only be a few minutes before the guards saw the empty car, stopped the train and formed a search. If we got into the first pastures away from the tracks, we'd add another mile of search radius to our benefit.

"KEEP RUNNING," Harry yelled. The grass was long and dry but turned green in front of us. A creek bed lead into a patch of woods. I couldn't do more to help other than trotting next to an elderly pair while holding their chains.

Odonna was behind me. "We'll regroup in those woods. That river's gotta lead us to a village." We kept chugging while listening for the train. It grew fainter. Every second compacted uncountable chances to find freedom. Woods were upon us.

"What about the rest of them?" I asked as we regrouped under a canopy of willows.

One of the elders looked perplexed, "Rest of who?"

"The slaves," I said.

Another older man said, "There's hundreds of thousands of us now. No one person, not you or anyone else, can free everyone. We hear the President is working on it. It might also lead to a war. It's one big mess."

Odonna agreed, "Yeah, but the only way anyone could clean it all up is to go way back in time, couple hundred years, before all this got started and stop the slave ships before they even landed from Africa."

The thought landed with the dull thud of little restoration for tired bones. Scars around ankles and wrists were far from healing. Shackles were far from being removed. I gave them a good run and fighting chance, but freedom was tenuous at best. Even if the train didn't stop short, they'd send cavalry from the next station. 44 slaves were too valuable to let slip away. It'd be like FedEx or UPS letting 44 delivery vans go flying over a cliff. Every business owner, even the ones depraved of every ethical and moral sense known to humanity, had to address their bottom line.

Harry put his hands on my shoulders. "Our little Wolf. Everyone on that train car today made it off. We are free. You did this for us. You freed us. What fate may be ours now is ours to choose."

"But I…"

"No but's. We thank you," he said.

The group huddled. Each methodically raised their head to give me a soft nod. Nothing more was said. But there was something else to do.

Again I asked Cat, "What would *you* do?" As I listened for Cat's answer, Odonna and I didn't break a stare. She knew I was talking to an invisible person.

I wondered, "Does she think I'm crazy? Hey, *her* plan is crazy."

And that's how it started.

11

Cat's Watch

It was getting dark so, naturally, the ceiling of my cargo container became filled with gum balls and LED lights. I developed an addiction for chewing from a bag of gum ball machine inserts. They were designed to cherish one at a time, with the clunk and roll of a dial and ramp. I chewed them like Doritos. At first I said to myself, "I need to create some adhesive for the lights." My mouth transformed into a dentist's dream.

I stuck another battery powered LED light on the ceiling with each chewed ball of goo. I had a wide variety at my disposal, from pucks to lines of Christmas lights. Some were timed off at night, just to keep a semblance of circadian rhythm. It was still dark during the day. Only my pinhole let in the sun's light. By the time I'd just ran out of stale bubble gum and LED's, my ceiling was alight in a multi-colored array. My skin even started to get a burn. So I removed a few to dim the heat of manufactured daylight, rotated some to take the stress off the batteries, and found a happy medium of light inside the container.

The temperature was getting difficult to manage. Before I left Earth's orbit, I'd oscillate between really hot and cold. I'd unpacked and flattened enough boxes to make a recycler very happy. Instead of breaking it down into re-usable pulp, the raw material would provide me a nice range of options. I built myself an insulation chamber by layering a dozen plies of cardboard around a bed-shaped cavity. I cracked the 10-packs of kid's glue sticks and burned through them. Truth be told, it looked like a disposable coffin. I even made a thick cardboard lid to pull over myself during the coldest hours of night and hottest hours of day.

I realized how much I was missing. "I need Wolf. I need her for everything. I need everyone for everything – for light, heat, water and food."

It was an exceptionally cold night up, floating and freezing alone in space, when it really started to dawn on me.

I was learning to survive on my own. I was getting pretty far away. There was also no further I could possibly go, separated from everyone, with no preparation with no prospect of ever seeing them again. Eventually the Amazon shipment bounty would run out. My resources would be depleted. All the brain power one individual could muster couldn't conjure invisible resources from (literally) thin air. The power of the many over the one was overtaking me. "I can't do it alone. No one can do *anything* alone."

Managing food, lighting and my temperature got even more complicated after my third orbit around Earth. I was graduating out of orbit. By my fifth rotation, our pale blue dot was getting as pale and blue as the chances of me returning home.

Seven "days" later, I was flinging further out into space. My time was passing differently than on Earth. Their days rotated neatly on the usual axis. I had no idea how to count anymore.

I tried keeping track of things with my yellow sticky notes and labels. The walls of the container were getting filled with scrawled Sharpie notes stuck in every corner with glue stick and gum ball bits. They started in an organized order, linearly tracking my minutes, hours and days. Then I stuck notes to each other, to create larger sheets for graphs and visual diagrams to track my movement.

I was looking for something else to write on.

The boxes stared back at me.

A can of worms opened, "Now there's a lot of writing surface." Fortunately I had enough fresh office pens to fill up all that brown paperboard.

"Would you like some breakfast?" My enlarged-snail-shaped robo-companion asked.

I felt obliged, "Uh, yeah, that sounds nice. Thanks BreakfastBot."

"My pleasure," he returned in a monotone voice. Indicator lights on his face slowly flashed colored light bars while contents churned in a pot-belly-like cauldron on his back.

"Black? Or cream? Sugar?"

I was impressed, "Wow, uh, just some cream I guess. Thanks BreakfastBot." The lid of the barbecue-like shell on his back lifted straight up. There was a hot plate of processed eggs and vegetarian bacon. A door slid straight up with a hot cup of coffee sitting in his mouth. I was grateful and mortified being fed and comforted by a cute little robot, "Thanks, BreakfastBot." It purred a little more as its inner servos and fans geared down. The cooing endeared me more. "For, like, everything, really, I guess," I confided.

He intoned his monotone delivery with a mock sense of excitement, "Brrrrrrreakfast is served!" I could see retro-style commercials advertising this guy being really effective. I smiled while eating my eggs. A bell dinged to indicate he was turning off.

I most track of things as my container exited the Earth's orbit on a trajectory away from the sun. I idly doodled around. I stopped my strict tracking logs.

I started using the square-shaped Post-It notes as origami paper. Wolf's Grandparents used to vacation in Japan and fell in love with the techniques. They brought home the fine paper to give as gifts. Wolf's Mom developed an appreciation for the art also. Wolf had a natural predisposition, being good with her hands. The paper just started folding itself in my hands. I remembered killing time in her room. I remembered her. It came to automatically. The paper creasing in my hand was bringing me closer.

I folded the shapes of things I once knew. I folded paper boats, cars, bears and people. I folded hamburgers, pizza slices, dandelions and birds. Buried deep in a lower box, somebody had ordered supplies to fill a tackle box. "Hmm, must've been for an office retreat or something. I never thought hanging the 'gone fishin' sign was a real thing." I used the fishing line to hang the origami.

My LED's twinkled color and cast shadows between the translucent folded paper. The cargo container shifted and rolled as it passed further from the sun. When I cruised past Saturn, I lurched a quarter angle to the side, so all the strings and origami's were cocked at an angle hanging from the ceiling.

Fifteen weeks passed, as best as I could estimate by the fledgling time-keeping I struggled to maintain. During this time, years were passing on Earth. I didn't know this exactly, but I knew I was missing a lot. I hoped, "Well, at least maybe that damn virus might be gone. But Wolf…"

What I didn't know was that the infections were raging wilder than ever. Mass volumes were being touched by minor infections — small circuit boards appearing on their abdomen, copper wires curling around ankles, copper tubes forming inside their intestine, neoprene hoses growing inside heart valves, buttons and toggle switches popping up behind ears. More than half of the world's population was infected. But, more than the ubiquity of the disease, the grotesque infections were terrifying.

Unchecked and untreated, wires, cables and switches formed more and more rivets, small metal doors and panels assembling on the body. Calves converted to pistons. Hips changed into hubs. Knees changed into ball bearings. Metal cabinetry would form around the torso and waist. Heads became toasters. People were systemically degrading into domestic appliances and calculating machines. Larger folks were turning into small cars, housing other infected people who were smaller and converted into electric and gas-powered engines.

There was no rhyme or reason. There was no discernible order or intention. If the robots (or evolutionarily advanced aliens, as the *real* conspiracy theorists were guessing) *were* really taking over, it was a stupidly sloppy way to do it.

Those severely infected – totally mutated into synthetic objects of autonomic purpose – performed their prescribed duties without any sense of grand plan or world domination. Formerly human, newly formed refrigerators cooled nothing but air. New desktop computers, of all shapes and sizes, mindlessly processed words, auto-played Solitaire games, and churned out the non-sensical search results of a Googling toddler or meth head. New cars drove to nowhere with no one inside. Audio mixers raised and lowered the levels of no sound at all. Oxygen machines pumped air for no one.

At some point I was doing nothing but folding little paper wolves. I stopped eating. I stopped counting. The water cooler refill reached stasis. The first refill that I'd already drunk and emptied – repurposed to seal my excrement inside – also reached stasis. A certain kind of equilibrium had been reached.

I pieced together rectangular adhesive folder labels into squares. I ripped 8 1/2 x 11 school paper into 8 x 8 squares. I ripped and de-corrugated the lids of cardboard boxes and tore those into squares too. I allocated all resources to folding more paper wolves.

I folded wolves at different sizes. I folded larger ones and used bits of my ABC gum to assemble to my other origami. Little origami birds and people were stuck on, riding the backs of larger origami wolves. I folded tinier wolves to stick into little pastel colored dioramas. Tiny wolves were climbing, walking and running through little origami trees and flowers. One little wolf sat in a boat.

I was starting to sleep for much longer periods of time. I brought my Wolf-in-a-boat into my insulation chamber. "Don't float away. Stay with me… Stay."

12

Wolf's Rage

<hr>

The children, their parents, sick and elderly left to find more safety. The rest travelled with me in a pack of 28. We had to get the shackles off.

The fear struck in the hearts of these people was wrong, from the deepest caverns of wrongness. I could feel the density of terror; the anticipation of search parties dispatched from the next train depot. In each furtive glance, in each motion to get free of the chains, I felt wrong, "I have to get back to the tracks."

Someone muttered, "You're crazy."

Odonna shushed, "No she's not."

Harry sided with her, "I'm going with you to help."

Odonna warned, "You better get moving. We all better move. They're probably on their way right now."

To a slave holder, there was no shame in devoting precious resources to reclaiming the loss of a valuable tool. Putting a bounty on the head of a runaway slave was as understandable as a Craigslist post to recover a stolen bike. It was a piece of machinery out of working order. Each cog had to be in place. Slave traders, even the crustiest ones who wouldn't lift a thumb from their shaded porch, were still weighted by the toll of labor. There have always been so many more efficient ways of making money.

If your hammer and nail kept running away from you, and these insubordinations inhibited you from building a house, it's time cut losses. Leave them be. Go find a better hammer and nail, ones that don't require a lack of humanity to use. It had nothing to do business or turning a profit. It was just evil. The calls for reparations were beginning to make sense to me in so many different ways. If it wasn't about making good money, they deserved to pay.

Folks had been separating themselves from each other for so many centuries that, when the robot cancer came around, they had no idea how to work together anymore. The disease could've been licked in a matter of weeks if everyone was just willing to work together and do the same thing. The infections would've stopped. Instead, the mechanical infections spread like wildfire because they were small enough for people to ignore; small enough for people to go about their lives; small enough for people who valued their personal liberty to forget entirely about everyone else around them. Even well educated people were spreading the disease. Even the people who should've known better failed to curtail the liberties they worked so hard to earn. Everyone was getting turned into photocopiers and inkjet printers. At least the disease was democratizing the world, even if those priding themselves on the philosophies of democracy weren't.

Harry helped me back to where we jumped. He readied me, "Next one should be coming. Wolf, my darling, remember your purpose here. You don't need to turn it all around. Remember - just you setting one car free already set all kinds of good wheels in motion." The tracks started to rumble. A whistle sounded, "You don't need to do much. Just be yourself. You don't need to change everything. One little thing can do it, just like you already did."

I thanked him as I prepared to go. "I'll never forget you, Harry. Tell Odonna I'll never forget her either!"

I took off running before the train came by. I caught up to a car with an open door and swung myself up inside. I climbed out and up to the top of the car. Once I got up there, I started running backwards again. I trucked and trucked, chugging in reverse of the train's motion. I hopped over gaps between cars and ran even harder. All I could see was the soft whiskers of my Kitty Cat's fast as the wind smashed against mine. It all turned into a rush.

Then the ground stopped moving again. I was running in place again. And POOF. It happened again. Just like the last time, I hadn't gone far. I was still in America. No, I hadn't travelled far in geographical terms. Again, it was the chronological variety of terms that had changed under my feet.

13

Cat's Descent

It was another infection: the thought overtaking my body. It wouldn't escape me, "I need Wolf."

I woke up to it in my insulation chamber. I fell asleep to the same thought. I wasn't just missing her face, her touch, her skin, her hair, eyes, hands and feet. I wasn't just missing her thoughts, her heart, soul, opinions and imperfections. I was missing more. "I'll never find the person who I want to be with. I'll never find anyone who's calm inside. Everyone's always bunched in knots in a hurry to do everything, even people I love. I am too. I'm the one. No one else will be. I have to be the person that I want to be with."

The issue wasn't that an independent cat emerging. If anything, it was saving me from going nuts. The real problem gnawed deeper inside that cargo container.

I was in space thousands of miles from Earth, while realizing how to cure the thing rampaging over it. I didn't know if, or when, I'd get back. If I did, I didn't know how I'd get people to listen. But at some point up there, floating alone in the cosmic void, it happened. It was about the same time you stop looking for the car keys when they're lost. It was when I least expected; when I'd nearly given up. When I felt the most systematically detached, it dawned on me, "I know it! I know how to do it." I realized *the why.* "Just one more thing to get over a tipping point. And I know she'll have it. AAAAAAAAAHH!!! I NEED WOLF!!!!!"

I fell into Jupiter's orbit around this time. At first I thought, "Great. Circling a gas giant for the rest of my life. That'll be great." But I didn't get stuck flying around that gassy mammoth. He just gave me a sling.

Nineteen "days" (again – to the best of my knowledge) later, I was on a straight trajectory back towards Earth. She was getting larger. Home was growing.

Returning toward Earth's orbit almost three weeks later, my container supplies were severely dwindled. I'd finished the Juicy Fruit, DoubleMint, gum balls, Red Vines buckets, not-hot Hot Pockets, not-tamale Hat Tamales, and barely peanut-butter peanut butter pretzels. I was into the last few inches of my last water cooler refill. There were two cans left of ninety-six soda vendor refills I'd tabulated at my wall of Sharpie-scrawled inventories. Remaining snacks and water would last a couple more days, then the clock would really tick.

"This will be your last meal before refill," BreakfastBot reminded me, yet again. I'd already switched out all the replacement cartridge heads that came with him. I rationed each meal he made and stretched them out into three or four. But the 3D-printed pancakes really didn't go down well if I didn't eat them right after they were made. And whoever ordered this guy didn't order extra cartridges. He must've been a gag.

He felt compelled to repeatedly warn me that his cartridge would run out before the last meal. "This will be your last meal before refill."

"It's nice of you to tell me, BreakfastBot, but…"

"This will be your last meal before refill."

"I know, but I'm gonna keep you on for now cause you can still make me coffee and I…"

"This will be your last meal before refill."

"…like the way you make me coffee."

He stopped talking. The indicator lights on the face of his cartridge angrily flashed yellow and orange. But he percolated and hummed along with his happy little sounds.

There were only so many iterations of the three main components the particular cartridge sets that came with him – pancakes, fake eggs and fake bacon. It was hard not to appreciate even his limited options, given the fervor and humor of his demeanor. He seemed to revel in his confined choices, *Do you want pancakes and eggs? Or do you want eggs and bacon? Or do you want bacon and pancakes?*

For the last meal he'd cook me, pancakes and bacon sizzled on his inner grill. He dinged, "Brrrrrrrreakfast is served!" Now all he had left to do now was serve me stale, watery coffee.

"Black? Or cream? Sugar?"

"Just cream, BreakfastBot. Thanks."

The door to his mouth opened with a fresh cup as he uttered, "You're welcome."

From the best I calculated with sticky notes and a dead cell phone – assuming my body still operated on a clock dictated by periodicity of Earth circling its sun - I had twelve days to live. I didn't just keep BreakfastBot on for the coffee. It was only an added bonus.

Jupiter's sling shot sent me into Earth's orbit at a good velocity. The cargo container settled into the circle around home. The fervor for sticky-note-tracking my trajectory reignited.

I feverishly traced lines and calculated timing, "I'm picking up speed!" Faster and faster I flew, until I neared the speed of the planet, only, in the opposite direction. I wondered, "If I can rig a catapult, I might hurl myself fast enough inside the container to match Earth's velocity."

I repurposed the springs, arms and levers of seven different brand new, un-assembled Herman Miller office chairs. I cleared a path through the middle of the container. I mounted the catapult at one end.

I checked my speed again with my Post-It notes and peephole, "Almost there! Time to mount up!"

I ran back to my catapult contraption and loaded myself in.

I calculated, "Seventeen seconds until I reach the exact same speed of Earth in reverse. Eight seconds to get mounted after leaving the peephole. Countdown nine… eight… seven…"

At zero, I released the catapult and sailed through the container at a thousand miles an hour.

It was a split second before my head decorated the wall like an abstract expressionist painting on the opposite end of the container. The entirety of everything vanished from the place where it was.

14

Wolf's Fang

I left Harry where I jumped from the 1800's. Again I trucked in the opposite direction the train travelled. Again the ground stopped and I vanished.

BAM! I fell on the ground. There was no train or tracks. "Uh, this won't be easy getting back home. Huh. What was I doing here?" In the distance was a coastline and sea port. A fleet of ships was sailing in. Docks prepared their arrival. "Oh yeah! I remember now."

I high-tailed it to the docks and ran into a group of colonists planning an attack.

"These guys are ruining everything," one of them whispered. He was twisting wicks, "We've got a militia here. We could use your help."

"I'm happy too. In fact, I came here for this reason," I exclaimed, "I thought I'd have to convince someone else to help!"

He packed another powder keg. "You know, kid, we have to fight off the Brit's and their corrupt monarchy trying to tax and control us from overseas. Now there's these idiots convinced that enslaving

Africans is the way to freedom. Don't they get it?! We're in the 1600's now! The Renaissance has happened! So many of us were born from it. We're supposed to be brilliant. Instead we're idiots! Idiots who think that freedom from the tyranny of British rule has nothing to do with every person, be they African or European, deserving freedom."

"Everybody wants to be free, I guess."

"NO!" He was on the verge of shouting. Four of his compatriots shushed him. He turned to whisper again, "Everybody wants freedom for *themselves*. They don't care about freedom for anyone else."

"Amen," I agreed, "want me to run those up for y'all?"

The militia men looked with a smile and shrug.

I explained, "I'm quick and strong, and I hate these guys more than you."

"You escaped?" One of them asked.

"In a way… sure."

"Then we'd be honored, young madame."

Another militia man bowed with a loaded keg in his hands. "We would be honored if you'd do us the service of disabling this ship arriving from the motherland."

The other men bowed, "We'll be right behind you."

I ran to the end of dock and chucked kegs out onto the ships before they pulled in. The explosions took out the salve traders. Those chained on board mounted a bloody fight. They killed their captors, freed themselves, swam ashore and helped us take out the remaining idiots running on the docks like chickens with their heads cut off. We cleared them out, then demolished the docks. We'd cut one head off, but knew that someday another would grow from the body of this demon. What we didn't know was that we set a new chain of events in motion.

I swam out to help the last freed prisoners onto shore. Militia men waded into the water to assist also. We'd blown the docks to pieces and slit the throat of the last ugly white man running from his horrible habit.

I climbed aboard one of the bombed out ships drifting a short distance from the docks. A slight gust caught the side of the hull and the ship turned. I surveyed the disarray on board, "What a mess." Blackened rubble was laid to waste. Bloodied bodies of men were strewn. Unchained shackles were tossed in piles.

Another gust caught and filled a sail. A wake trailed. I scanned the carnage of our rampage, "I can't believe these men would give their own skin to trade another man's." The wind picked up again.

I looked up and the dock was straight off the stern, a half mile away. The ship was sailing itself out on a solid clip into the wind. "Uh, that's no good. I gotta get back!"

I bolted towards the stern from the bow.

And there it happened again: right then, just before I launched into the water off the back of the ship. In the opposite direction, I was running at the same speed that the ship was sailing. Relative to me, the water stopped moving, and POOF - I was gone again.

15

Cat's Tracks

I was sinking back down to Earth. My container full of unpacked Amazon shipments and survivalist decorations was returning. I was landing on the tracks where I left Wolf, but I didn't land on a moving train.

The cargo container eased down, and slowed and slowed. I reached a turtle's pace just before touching down. I landed on the tracks with a dull and unglamorous, "THUD."

The landing rattled BreakfastBot's cartridge contents. The indicator lights on the face of cartridge furtively flashed as if he wasn't empty, "This will be your last meal before refill."

I reminded him, "You already served me the last meal, BreakfastBot."

Then he sadly repeated his more recently familiar refrain, "Please change my cartridge. I have no breakfast to serve. Please change my cartridge."

At first, the subtle movements of floating in space were impossible to shake. "I can't believe I'm on the ground again." My sea legs were wobbly. I tried standing up and fell right back down. I could only sit.

I tried taking in a deep breath of air. The rich air overwhelmed my starved lungs; the cool humidity of water vapor filled every breath. It was Earth all right, our gloriously wet planet. Even in a sealed cargo container, you can tell that the air is full of it. I never realized how dehydrated I'd become up in space.

Trying to stand was a mistake. Trying to breath was bad too. It all hit me at once.

Then I passed out.

CREEEEEEEEK.

Local authorities were opening my heavy, rusted, squeaky cargo containers doors. The sound of the doors woke me up. The authorities happening upon me were gifted quite a sight.

Inside this container, set perpendicular on tracks across the unremarkable stretch of middle America plains where our homes were made, lay a young cat passed out napping on his back. I didn't make it in my insulation chamber before crashing on the floor with my arms splayed out. I must've looked dead. All evidence would've pointed to that conclusion.

Locals caught sight of my container descending from the sky. The internet had exploded with rumors before I landed. The authorities who saw the footage wasted no time setting up an elaborate rescue opp. Cameras and gawkers were already there.

Seven years prior, Wolf and I's parents had sent word that their children were lost. Search parties had been sent but so much attention was fixed on the cancer. After Earth circled its sun seven times, fatigue and exhaustion were giving way to pandemonium.

The search for a cure or vaccine revealed no prospects. Our parents gave up on the search too. So many were being lost. Infections were running amok, wantonly turning people into television sets, nightlights, alarm clocks, boomboxes, modems and server banks. It wasn't irresponsible for a parent to safely assume their child had become an inanimate, nameless, lifeless piece of technology sitting on a street corner somewhere, lighting an intersection or controlling traffic with mindlessly flashing lights.

NASA had been watching an object floating in space that appeared to be a run-of-the-mill cargo container temporarily orbiting Earth. They had begun to make preparations for a more intensive investigation, perhaps even a search party or shuttle mission as I'd suspected. But again, everyone's attention was so focused on the virus. It was too hard to get other balls rolling.

A rescue worker asked, "Son? You ok?"

Television cameras were alight. Microphones pressed into the crowd surrounding the open cargo doors. Helicopters whirled overhead.

"I think he's dead," someone whispered.

Hardly anyone thought about how the cameras, microphones and helicopters could've recently been people who'd undergone total metamorphosis after being infected by the cancer. Attention spans had switched. Apparently it *wasn't* hard to get other balls rolling, as long as it was a juicy ball.

"This just in: Boy found unconscious inside train car floated in from space!" A reporter narrated, "More at 11."

Finding that cargo container, in the middle of nowhere or anywhere else, was a welcome bit of news and relief, and not just for our families. Any odd sign of hope was an international blessing. Anything, any distraction, any shift in the monotonous dynamic that had taken hold of every facet of life, to take people's minds off a grueling seven-year battle with raging infections, was more than a blessing. It was a news story to end all the other depressing news stories. It was an eccentric treasure. And it was a miracle.

Plus, Wolf had been changing history back in time. She was busy pumping the prime of humanity for a wholly different trajectory altogether. Things were about to change. Opening those heavy doors to find me inside was just icing on the cake for a world in which more than half the population had been lost to technological devices. I was a celebrity before anyone even knew there was a person inside my container.

After living in it for months, finding the state of my container's interior was another story.

16

Wolf's Return

Instead of landing in the water off the back of that bombed slave ship, I landed on another train in the year 2024. I recognized cars and familiar sites. At first I thought, "I'm back home!" The train was at the edge of town and slowing. I tumbled off, brushed myself down and started to making sense of what I was seeing.

I was home, but seven years had passed. The infections had annihilated the home I once knew. I was back in the place where I once belonged. It was the place where I was raised. It was <u>not</u> the place I knew when I left. I jumped off the train at the edge of town to eery sites on every corner.

Brand new video cameras and turntables were stacked next to unused defibrillators and portable freezer units. Utility lines hung over intersections were littered with dozens of traffic lights. Our town was never big enough to warrant more than three lights. And they were spread out to the ends of town. The stop lights had hatched like spiders from a healthy nest, wantonly reproducing, meandering down phone lines, appearing away from intersections, and blinking at unintelligible intervals.

A table saw with an un-rusted, razor sharp blade sat in the middle of an intersection. A large 3D-printer was left on its side, blocking the doorway to the laundromat. The laundromat had been shuttered. The door was sealed in. We were a one-laundromat town with a half dozen machines that, maintained properly, would serve everyone well, even on a busy Saturday. It was not this way inside. Sure it looked busy, but it was no Saturday afternoon. No one was there. It was just washers and dryers stacked floor to ceiling, wall to wall, filling every inch of the place.

A cellophane vacuum-sealing machine was parked squarely at the head of the handicap spot outside the laundromat.

Five 1980's boomboxes were pressed together, pounding out music from inside a Prius parked diagonally on top of a concrete bench next to the bus stop.

A digital camera was stuck sitting on a forgotten stoop, errantly and endlessly snapping pictures of the same two stair steps over and over again.

I walked out of town, towards my house and along the tracks with one thing on my mind, *"He's got to be here."* Office Depot was like the laundromat, but super-sized. It'd been closed for years. Computers, printers and copy machines were pressed against the inside of every storefront window and covered in dust. Home Depot was no different. They'd all been out of business a long time.

It made sense. A cornucopia of anything you'd want to buy in those stores would sit on the corner outside your house, free, new and unused.

It got even more depressing after I passed the shuttered strip malls and big box stores.

Long-defunct devices sat outside nursing homes and halfway houses. Cluttered in rows were never-been-used VCR's, cassette players, GameBoys, Disc-men, Walkmen, classic NES consoles and 8-track players. It was like the Christmas dream of a Gen-X kid; some late 20th Century shopping spree gone wild. Except, all of the joy and hope of seeing these once-coveted gadgets of desire conjured the opposite feelings.

A mile from my house, I stopped to rest by a crystal clear, 48-inch flat screen sitting on the ground outside corner store. It was tilted at an angle with a TV news commentator lamenting, "Uninfected populations continue to act as though nothing is wrong, gathering in large groups and congregating at theaters and parties. While other towns have been decimated, some with over three quarters of the population having passed the virus - secreted in skin oils and vaporized in vocal cavities - readily amongst the community until entire streets of small town America are reduced to nothing more than row after row of technological gadgets and gizmos… And now, a message from our sponsor."

Apple's business had been cut in half. No one needed an iPhone or iPad. They were likely to grow one in place of their hand if they really wanted. Sony, Dell, Magnavox, Samsung, Panasonic, GE and all the others had folded. Droves of Chinese and Japanese manufacturing facilities screeched to a halt.

Even life online had slowed to a snail's pace. It was getting more and more difficult to access that world. Infected people were turning into devices that might normally be used to game, stream or network. But these newly formed devices weren't necessarily connected, activated, plugged in or charged. They'd just create themselves from the flesh of a human body, then sit there wherever they were created. It still took a human to operate and network these things. There were less and less of these operators around, growing rarer by the day.

Two people were yelling at each other at the end of the block before my house. The woman kept encroaching. The frumpy-looking man kept backing away.

The woman's expensive bracelets shook as she waved her arms. "You can't *see* me give it to you can you? No! That's because it's not me!! It's THEM. They're giving it to you. *They're* the ones making you sick. Not me! No way!"

The frumpy guy tripped on his baggy sweatpants as he backed off more. "Look - I can't do what I want because you're just doing whatever you want. I wanna hang out with my friends. I wanna see my family. I wanna go to the bar. But I can't do that because of people like *you*!"

The woman argued, "Well you should just do whatever you want! That's what I'm doing. And I'm having a great time. Look at me - I'm happy!"

The man stopped ceding ground, "You're giving me THIS!" She backed off a half step at the sight of vinyl hoses and slender coaxial cables puncturing his neck. Then he pulled his dingy bath robe open. A camera lens had formed from his right nipple. A video monitor had grown over his left pectoral. "DOES *THIS* MAKE YOU HAPPY?!?!"

She rationalized, "You could got that from anywhere… processed foods, the drinking water, hell, your own doctor, or outer space. I don't know! All I know is you didn't get it from me. It ain't my fault!"

As she relented and turned to leave, the man noticed something, "LOOK AT YOUR LEGS!" Fiberoptic lines matched varicose veins and pantyhose stitches tracing patterns down the back of her thighs and calves.

"I DON'T CARE!" She yelled back, "I'D RATHER GO THIS WAY THAN LIVE MY LIFE IN FEAR!"

My house was empty - of people, that is. I couldn't tell how new or old our household appliances and devices were. I couldn't tell if they'd been used. We didn't have much to begin with. I couldn't tell if my parents had just been there, if they were out looking for me, or just away working at the deli. It was the middle of the day and normally Dad would be sitting there, half sauced, glued to the TV. It did look like a newer flatscreen. That would've made sense for Dad if he was still alive, I guess. At some point there would've been an upgrade. Maybe he did. Maybe he was speaking to me.

The pixelated local news anchor was interrupted by bad reception, "…'fections now triple what they were at this point last year. Please note… 'pared to just two weeks ago, you are 100% more likely to mutate if you go out. Please, do not tr… "

The microwave dinged. Nothing was cooking. It hadn't even been on. The clock just flashed "12:00" as if there'd been a power outage. Then it dinged again.

I often wondered what microwaves were thinking and feeling when you set the timer for 30 seconds, pulled out a thawed muffin 3 seconds early, then closed the door and let those last 3 seconds just sit there. The microwave would dutifully sit there all day flashing those last 3 seconds. It'd never waiver. It wouldn't ask you to reset. It wouldn't even bother you. It'd just sit and wait until you needed it again for another reason. It'd just flash and flash those 3 seconds forever.

"Good microwave," I reinforced. It dinged again, right before I patted it on top. Then it dinged twice more. Then I pulled the plug. Then it dinged again.

It wasn't just the ghosts in the machines. The house was an altogether sad and horrifying place. I wanted to check the deli for Mom.

Outside the door of my house, I paused on the porch, then ran through the front yard. I ducked my head past the half-human, cyborg terrors staring me down. I took off down the street and arrived at the deli in record time.

It looked quiet form the outside. I got closer and noticed the door was ajar. Mom never left it unlocked. Right before I put my hand on the door to open it, something rustled inside. Then there was a CLUNK and something hit the shelves. It wasn't small.

Looting and pillaging had become commonplace in the seven years that passed while I was lallygagging back in time. Store owners and clerks were morphing into Slurpie dispensers and soda fountains. Even for shop owners who managed to stay open (and alive), a thick air of lawlessness had settled in while I was gone, like unwelcome alley cat. Police officers standing and steady on the beat right there in the street, were contracting, folding in on themselves and converting into CB radios and stun guns. No one would come to the rescue, no one answered 911 calls, no regulation, enforcement or holding anyone to account for anything, even if there were laws governing the land. State houses, governor's mansions and federal court buildings had all been ravaged too.

The big living thing inside Mom's deli bumped another shelf. THUD.

"Someone's inside. But Mom would've locked the door, even if she was inside." I knew, "She'd lock herself inside forever before ever leaving that door unlocked."

BAM. Something fell from another shelf. My hand was frozen an inch from touching the door. Old posts, worn out stickers and the scuffs of endless activity obscured the door's glass windows. I couldn't see much inside. "I'm pretty sure they can't see me," I reassured myself.

Grandma was shot and killed by a shoplifter. It was back in Korea, in their shop. Mom saw the whole thing. Hence the door locking rituals.

Mom also learned not to shy away, either. And it was part of her befriending the train-hopping hobos - she knew that if she cultivated relationships with certain vagabonds and transients, she'd get a better understanding of the culture and, therefore, her enemy.

I asked myself, "What would Mom do?"

The answer was obvious.

I placed my hand on the door and slowly pushed it open. I had no idea if I'd encounter an armed robber, cowering child, or rutting bear.

The door crept open. All went silent.

"Hello?" I vocalized timidly.

No answer.

Then, "THUD." A box fell off a low shelf.

A man in a dark overcoat jumped up, "Don't shoot! I'm unarmed!"

"So am I!" I conferred over the eye-level shelf dividing us between deli aisles.

"Good. Then you won't mind helping me," he pronounced calmly. That's when the shot gun appeared. He slowly pulled it from under his arm to present as a threat. My body shuttered with a new, but all too familiar, fear.

I raised my empty palms, "Ok, look. I'll do whatever you want. Just, let's stay calm."

"Good, then help me fill up my bag. There's gotta be some batteries in some of these boxes," he gestured to the closed and unmarked supplies sitting on the shelves.

I didn't say anything while turning to open a box and look for batteries. He watched me a second, then turned to look in another box. I kept acting like I was looking, "You know, this was my Mom's shop."

"Uh huh," he mumbled without interest.

"I think I can remember where she'd put them," I peaked at him under my box-rummaging arms. The right hand on his gun flashing with metal.

"I don't care who you are, kid. You could just be trying to pull one over on me. Just keep looking," he directed without diverting his attention from the boxes. He just kept digging without looking up at me. The metal on his gun-toting hand extended up his wrist and well up his arm. Every time he rifled around in another box, his coat sloshed and more became visible. Then it became visible on his abdomen and back.

"Yeah, well, uh, I think I can pretty much remember where she put everything," I guessed, trying to buy myself time, "if I can just think about it for a sec."

"DON'T THINK! AND STOP TALKING!" He shouted. Then he swung the gun tip at me, "JUST KEEP LOOKING!"

I froze in terror. I couldn't tell which was worse. The shot gun aimed at my face was half of it. The paper thin titanium and aluminum sheets crawling up his neck were the other half. He neck muscles bulging in anger as he seated at me. The metal foil wrapped over the bulging muscles, reflected and amplified the up and down motions a moment, then cooled, cured and hardened on his neck. He gasped as the new metal singed on his neck. The gun lowered.

I looked straight at him, "That's not gonna get any better."

"SHUT UP!" He was far less than ten feet away and we were indoors. The deli door had wedged open and we weren't far inside. But I'd taken my last breath a while prior.

The armed shoplifter stumbled back away from me, deeper into the store. His gun dropped to the ground. I backed away and stepped outside the open deli door.

Cables looped up behind his ears. The tendrils of low voltage cords slid silently under his chin, up towards his face. Servos and motors were replacing the joints in his fingers. Skin and muscles wilted, dried and fell to the floor. It was told that there was a significant heat that resonated from the victim of robot cancer. All the new electrical energy would radiate and heat the victim's living tissue to such a point that it'd just fall right off like ashes from a burning log.

From the outside of the shop, I spoke to him laying and writhing on the deli's hard formica floor in the pain of his infection. I confronted him at a distance, "Yeah, actually, if I think about for a sec, I can remember just about everything from my Mom's deli. And more! I remember how her Mom was shot and killed in *her* deli back in Korea."

The armed robber's shoes were torn off by cast steel wheels forming in the place of his feet. His legs bent inward. His knees folded backward. Then each of his legs folded twice again in places you never want to see a leg fold. His limbs were accordion-folding onto themselves and flattening to press against his body. The springs, pistons and ball bearings of swivel joints appeared at the pivot point of each new fold in his body.

He kept recoiling too. He used his last strength to shimmy himself down the aisle, away from me. The shot gun, laying on the floor, had gotten further away from him too. It had come between us, more than ten from him. He kept scooting down the aisle, deeper into the store. I stepped back in.

"And she told me that if I ever had to defend myself," I continued, "I should."

I leaned down, picked up the shot gun, lifted it, and aimed it at the robber more than fifteen feet away from me, inside the shop. His coat had fallen off. A small portion of his shirt was the only piece of his clothing remaining on his body. Four circuit boards filled the area of his torso and back. His legs had folded into a series of tightly closed metal slats. His whole body had contracted to half its size.

I lined up the scope, "I could blow you away right now."

"PLEASE! Do it! Help me! Kill me now!" He mustered from the last bits of unmechanized mouth he could operate. Radiator grills had wrapped around his cheeks and jaw. Ears became gears. His skull flattened to a perfect plane on the top and bottom.

The trigger was resting in my finger, "Wait a minute… you were just touching this." I dropped the gun and stepped back.

He tried to manage one more plead, but all he could get out was, "PLEE….."

The flat planes of his head narrowed in on themselves. His body shrunk even more. He kept getting smaller and smaller, shorter and shorter, flatter and flatter, metal-er and metal-er.

I backed myself out of the shop and turned to go. I glanced back right before getting out of sight. The guy had become a Roomba.

The world fast-forwarded seven years had not progressed. It wasn't like things had fast-forwarded seven years at all, actually. It was more like the world had just been placed on pause, then unpaused again when I jumped in time, off that bombed out slave ship. A fast forward would have indicated that something had been fast-forwarded through. But it was like nothing had happened. No time had passed. Nothing had changed. It was all right where we left it: people just getting decimated, over and over again, by the robot cancer.

I had to find my lost Cat.

17

Cat's Cradle

Walls were plastered with Post-It notes, labels and 3-hole-punched school paper. The ceiling was full of gum-hung LED lights. Boxes were arranged in peculiar patterns. Notes were scribbled over every bit of cardboard.

Origami wolves were littered everywhere. They were in little scenes, on top of things, inside other things. They were stacked on top of each other, one after another, until they couldn't be stacked any higher.

The first thing that came out of my mouth when I came to: "Dude - you people need to spread out!"

"You're right, son," the rescue worker helping revive me noted. He stepped out and called, "All right everyone back! Y'all need to back up and step away from the container! Everyone spread out!" He cleared the cameras, reporters and other first responders. They spaced themselves out at the ten foot intervals, safe to prevent the spread of infection. No one was visibly infected, but it was too often hard to tell.

The rescue worker stepped back toward the container and stopped short of the open doors. I was still on the floor. My throat was hoarse. I spoke softly, "Thank you. It's like you guys don't even care about trying to stop this thing anymore. Nice to see some effort."

He was a little triggered, "We're just totally fatigued. You know, those of us who care have worked so hard for so long, and sacrificed so much. Those of us who don't care – who think the whole thing is some elaborate conspiracy by space aliens, bored billionaires, or big tech companies – well, they just never tried to stop it at all. They all keep spreading the disease without a care in the world. I mean, say – everyone's just imagining and fabricating this thing and it's all a hoax. Then even the conspiracy theorists are in on it, and they're the worst. They embolden everyone else who *does* believe that it's even more terrifying. It's all one big shit show."

"Won't be for long," I forced from my lips.

"What's that, Cat?"

"How'd you know my name?"

"Kid, you're famous. We saw you coming down. People pieced it together pretty quick. You're one of those two kids who disappeared from the tracks seven years ago, just after the infections started… *The Disappearance of Cat & Wolf*… didn't you see the Nightline story… well, I guess you couldn't, well… it sure is good to see you, Cat. There's never been a better site for sorer eyes! You've lifted our spirits."

As we spoke, memes were ablaze about the cat on the tracks, things getting stopped in their tracks, Black cats crossing paths, and such. Pictures of my cargo container sitting there by itself, detached from a train and perpendicular on the tracks, were readily shared and Photoshopped. Some nicknamed me "The Magic Cat." Others tagged "CAT GOT YOUR TONGUE?" Because I hadn't spoken to anyone but the rescue worker.

I'd been on the ground for less than hour. Bloggers, reporters, influencers and amateur photographers were rapidly descending on the scene. It was the best and weirdest (albeit at the tail end of a worldwide robot cancer outbreak) news anyone had since the infections started. Seven long years were coming to a head. The world was waiting on bated breath to hear what I had to say. I wanted to know if my Mom was ok, but all I could think about was *her*.

The rescue worker cleared space for me to step into the light outside the container. Solid ground still did not feel that way. I almost bit it.

"Woah, Cat man," the worker warned me and my wobbly legs, "You gotta let yourself adjust. I won't break the plane to hold you. We'll keep our ten feet. You gotta do this one on your own."

"I'm used to that."

"I'm sure you are. But you gotta take it easy. Take your time. The world can wait."

I condescended, "No it can't." I had plans and visions. I had solutions and cures, "I know how to solve this."

A question came from a news reporter standing twenty feet away, "You know *what*, young man?"

For all my lofty ambitions, for all the wisdom I wanted to share, the words out of my mouth were, "Do you know if she's ok?"

"Haven't heard yet, kid," the reporter angled away from me and toward the camera, "And there you have it, folks: right here, from the cat's mouth. He just wants to know where his girlfriend is. If that's not true love, I don't know what is. Doesn't it just break your heart, Liz?"

The reporter pressed her earphone to listen for Liz's response. I didn't care what it was. I was serious. I wanted to know where Wolf was. It would take almost a day before I'd get an answer. And things were just beginning to mount in that day. My fame was drawing a lot of attention. It started to get pretty strange.

People starting pouring in from neighboring towns and counties. Then they came from neighboring states. Then they came from the north and south. Soon they'd start coming from the air. Some particular visitors stood out.

About an hour after they opened my doors, Michael Jordan walked up with an entourage.

"Hey Cat," he said nonchalantly, like I could just say hi to Michael Jordan right back.

"Um, wow," I was disoriented, "Hello?!"

"I had to come see you. I remember the story about you and your girl disappearing. I couldn't forget it, especially when I heard it was only a couple hours from where I live," Michael explained. His diction and demeanor were comforting. I'm sure he saw my shoulders relax before going on, "So when I saw this… *thing*… come down from the sky, I knew exactly what it was and we just hopped in the car immediately. I had to come see for myself."

"Wow. Well, um, Mr. Jordan, I, um…"

"Call me Michael."

"Wow. Thank you… Michael," I snickered. "I'm just so blessed…. I'm, um, honored, really. That you remembered us and came here. Can't believe it, really."

"Well, you better believe it," he stated, "Because I'm here."

"God, Michael. I have no idea what to say. I'm pretty overwhelmed, you know? Like, what would you say to Michael Jordan if you ever had the chance to meet him?"

"Yeah," Michael smiled, "What would you say?"

"I don't know. I guess I still think about what happened to your pops. I'd tell you I'm sorry. I'd wanna know how it's been for you. I just feel like we all went through that with you together. And that alone must have been tough. You couldn't grieve for him yourself. You had to deal with everyone else's grief for you and your Dad, and you never had a chance to," I stopped. Tears were welling up and Michael's eyes were turning red. "Oh God - I didn't mean to…"

"No no. It's ok," Michael told me while wiping his eyes. "No one's asked me about him in a long time. I think about him all the time, every day. I think about everything he told me, all the things he taught me. And then all this time passes, people stop asking about him, and you think that everyone's kinda just forgotten about him. But I still think about him all the time, you know?"

I held Michael's glare longer than he did. I'd ripped open a wound. Then I felt mine reopen too.

I confessed, "Well, actually, no, I don't. Mine left when I was too young to remember him. I think about him a lot, probably every day. But at this point it's just a fabricated fantasy that I've constructed in my head."

Michael stopped crying and wiping his face. Then he held my gaze longer than I held his. "I know I'm not supposed to break the plane here. But I just want you to know that I'd hold your chin up right now if I could," he said.

"Thanks, man," then *I* started crying, "My Mom's been great, really great. Like, as good as it gets. But it's different coming from a man, you know?"

"I know."

"I can tell you're a great father," I told him.

Michael's grin forced more tears back inside. "I'm gonna leave you now, Cat. But it's not for long. I'll come back and visit. That's a fact."

"I believe you."

And with that, Michael Jordan left me. His entourage followed along as he disappeared into the crowd.

It's one thing to share more than the moment surrounding an autograph signing or obligatory handshake with a celebrity. It's another thing to share that kind of moment with someone on a superhuman level. But the *kind* of moment we shared was transcendent. I know I'll never forget it. Somehow I feel like Michael won't forget it either.

That's *crazy*, right? Michael Jordan won't forget me? Forget about it.

18

Wolf's Charade

Even if I found Cat, we'd have to quarantine for three weeks. I had no idea where he was or where he'd been. I could only tell that some seven years had passed while I was off galavanting in the 17th and 19th Centuries. I groaned, "What was it all for if I can't see him again?"

I approached the tracks. "No trains coming. Guess I'm walking it." I started putting things together as I strode the rails. Words and ideas swirled into a beautiful mess in my head.

Tracks stretched into the distance. "Still no train in sight." Then a small clump appeared. It was too wide to be a train. It grew as I got closer. Beings moved around. "Could it be? It *has* to be!"

I rolled onto the scene in a huff. People were dispersed in clumps around the open cargo container. There he was, sitting on the edge of the open doorway.

I was fifty feet away and immediately burst into tears. He hadn't seen me yet.

There, sitting next to my Cat, was LeVar Burton. Like, *the* LeVar Burton. The-Roots-Reading-Rainbow-

Geordi-LaForge LeVar Burton. That LeVar Burton. Multiple circles were coming full circle.

LeVar was effectively interviewing Cat, sitting a good distance away, with cameras and microphones broadcasting their conversation live for the crowd that had congregated, and beyond. I'd walked close enough to make out some of what they were saying just by reading their lips. I was close enough to see my lovers lips.

LeVar asked Cat, "Have you seen any of your family?"

"I haven't been able to see anyone I love," Cat cried, "I can't… I just can't…"

Cat stood up to walk away but LeVar kept going, "You've got to tell your story. Make them hear you."

Cat stopped.

LeVar yelled, "Tell them what you just told me before we starting rolling the camera!"

Cat turned back toward LeVar. I slowly stepped closer. Cat and LeVar continued talking. Cat stumbled for words. LeVar caught his fall.

Those standing nearby knew who I was (I guess that Nightline episode was getting a lot of replay). They parted a clear path between us. Wolf and I could see each other, but he still hadn't seen me. The crowd wanted the scene to be made for TV. They were a part of it. They were there; history in the making. Everyone on the scene became a director choreographing a reality broadcast back to the masses.

Cat's head turned away from LeVar. His eyes met mine. His body lifted. He screamed through his tears, "Come!"

I ran and stopped, "I can't come closer!"

He yelled with wet joy and sorrow, "AAAAAAAAHHHH!!!!" His head angled back and his voice cracked and he screamed again.

I shouted too, "I LAAAAAAAAAAHHHHVE YOU!!! MY KITTY CAAAAAAAT!!!!"

We stood more than ten feet apart. His art installation cargo container sat crosswise on the tracks behind him. Hyper-aware, choreographing, photographing and uploading onlookers went quiet. LeVar Burton stood and stared too. Even Georgi La Forge was at a loss for words. All cameras rolled, including the ones not being operated by anyone.

I circled Cat's container, "You did all this? Kitty Cat, it's amaaaaaazing." To see so much beauty he'd produced, I could only imagine how much pain he'd endured, "Where have been and what did you do? Were you stuck in there this whole time?"

"Wolfie, I have a thousand questions for you too."

I pealed my eyes from the splendor my Cat had constructed in his traveling container. We knelt and faced each other near the container. We barely blinked. LeVar Burton walked off. Then the onlookers started firing questions.

Days passed with Cat and I sitting there on the tracks, twelve feet away from each other. Our fame only grew. Reporters and bloggers kept firing away. Multiple live streams opened up a set of competing Truman Shows. Good folks brought us food, sleeping pads, and blankets.

At night we just laid there. I'd rest on my side and put my head on the rail. He'd lay on his stomach and rest his head to face me. We talked until we fell asleep, and woke up in the same positions.

On our third day of publicly exposed quarantine, volunteer carpenters and furniture makers used remote-controlled fork lifts to bring us makeshift beds that fit squarely in the train tracks. They used cranes to remotely erect tents around us. The tents were fashioned with circle-top doors that allowed Cat and I to face each other with nothing between us.

At that point in Summer around our town, the weather was warm and dry. We could outside all night and be totally fine. Our nights romping in the fields after jumping 4 a.m. trains had proven it beyond a shadow of a doubt. 28 seasons had passed but we'd been put right back where we were left, in the same place at the same time of year, just seven of them later.

We answered as many questions from the crowds that we could. Questions were hurled from more than ten feet away. Speakers and more microphones were brought in. They left us alone when we asked, so Wolf and I could reconnect, bond, commiserate and catch up on what we'd missed.

It was so hard not to touch him, not to feel his skin. I wanted the fine details of his face with my eyes, the surface texture of his back, the new moles on his stomach, the imperfections of color and shape in his irises. I wanted his hands on me. I wanted his mouth on me. He wanted the same.

But as much as we wanted each other, as much love as we felt re-firing in every corner of our bodies, as much as we were closing the gaps between us, there was an inescapable feeling to the contrary.

Without naming it, we both had a suspicion that we'd grown apart. We'd both been so far and seen so much. Even though he was stuck sealed inside a metal box by himself, Cat had seen the earth from afar. He'd faced demons and his own fate. He was confronted with a perspective that he brought back home to inspire the world. The lone Cat – so self-reliant and proud, able to fend for himself without anyone else's help – was haphazardly motivating the world towards a collective mindset.

They halted all trains on the route. International news media converged. A tent city (metropolis, really) sprouted up, replete with its own cottage industry of vendors hawking wares. T-shirts, mugs and felted animals adorned with our faces were being sold. Paper wolves became an international symbol of unified solidarity to end the cancer. People camped in clumps around media and vendor tents. Everyone diligently spaced their bubbles more than ten feet apart. We didn't even have to remind them.

Even the homegrown DIY vendors selling tchotchkes and snacks to campers who'd pilgrimaged to the site to see Cat and I – even they were being responsible and only taking orders online through mobile devices. They were making everyone pick up their goods at equally spaced relay stations. The whole site was becoming a replicable template to upscale across communities in every corner of the planet. Burning Man had nothing on us. That desert party annually ended in a pile of trash with everyone going back to their climate-destroying desk jobs. *This* was how to save the world. We were showing them, and they were showing us. The love between us, rumbling on ten feet of track separating us, was so pure it was impossible not to ingest. Our love was so visibly raw - with us laying there on train tracks day in, day out for twenty-one days, like star-crossed lovers willing to commit mutual suicide for each other - people were seeing truths that were invisible before.

They saw two young lovers in love, wanting nothing more than to be together, but sacrificing and separating from each other just to kill the disease and save the world. That's what *they* saw. What they didn't see was what was inside us. It was all one big charade.

19

Cat's Tongue

"Our reunion happened just a few feet away from 'our spot' where we'd sneak out, jump trains and meet in high school," Wolf told a live-streaming influencer.

I grinned and rolled my eyes, "Well, not exactly, Wolfie."

When the influencer looked to me, Wolf playfully gestured to shush and silently pantomimed, *"It's good for the show."*

"Actually – she's right – I forgot. It *was* just over there. Wolfie's always right," I told the influencer. The streaming influencer looked back to Wolf. I continued our game of charades behind the influencer's back, *"We're saving the world!"* Luckily the well-intentioned girl, who was doing the good work of promoting the cause, kept turning her phone camera so she didn't see our little Cat and Wolf game.

The influencer was savvy to reclaim the interview's reigns. "I guess I never knew cats and wolves got along so well, huh?" The soft ball allowed her to pivot and reference the next question from an earlier part in the interview about the sacrifices people were making. She dug in, "So seriously, Cat: you think you know what everyone needs to do to cure the disease? You think you know more than all the world's best scientists? You think you've figured something out on your own in a few months that no one on Earth has figured out in seven years?"

"Well, the disease is still running rough shot, isn't it?"

She couldn't deny the logic of the frame. "True enough."

I went for it, "I think a lot of people spend a lot of time doing things they know they shouldn't, and telling themselves stories about why it's ok. Even people who come close to practicing what they preach still have to cut corners just to get by. And if they preach about practicing what they preach, they're snobs. It's like: integrity is a pariah, a myth, or luxury. Most don't have resources to even consider it. Most people spend all day picking battles, contradicting themselves, or choosing the lesser of two evils. That's life."

Wolf intervened, "It's like, there's always something to complain about. Even the richest, most privileged assholes on Earth whine all the time. It's gratitude over grief, you know?"

I couldn't help but oversimplify, "People know what to do. They just have to do it."

After signing off with her fans, the influencer confided, "Your candor is doing this, you know. You two are being so real, so honest, and it's rubbing off."

The international pilgrimage to Wolf and I's reunion site reached a fever pitch around the eighteenth day of quarantine. Tents, mobile homes, campers, trucks, vans, and homemade huts were stationed apart as far as we could see. Estimates ranged between a million or two had safely assembled around us.

My cargo container was being hailed as a historical artifact of profound significance. Famous architects were enlisted to discern the meanings of my cardboard box arrangements. Art historians and curators were throwing around fancy language, coin words and buzzy linguistics to describe my chamber. The art people especially loved that, *"The work was done by a person of color."* They made note of it as much as they could, as if making note of it was some sort of laudable and noble act on its own. Even the state of my water cooler refill excrement containers (sealed so they didn't smell) was being vaulted as some sort of important, ethnographic, performance art milestone. This wasn't mere token-izing. The art people weren't just making amends. They were bending themselves over backwards. Some of them were literally doing this, just to get a better look at things.

AI researchers visited to field study BreakfastBot on-site. Many were convinced that it was his psychological components, not just his culinary craft, that saved my life. All I know is I stayed alive weeks after he stopped making food, without eating anything else. All he did was remind me that he needed to be refilled. He just needed more.

CNN, NBC and FoxNews had staged a press conference with microphones and cameras remotely propped for Wolf and I to do a live, split-screen interview with reporters.

A reporter lead, "You're being called – not just the leaders of a generation – but the leaders of a new world, a world free of robot cancer. Infections are down, circuit boards, combustion chambers and copper wires are leaving our skin, but there is still a long way to go. Much of the world is still highly infected, with many communities and sub-cultures still deeply entrenched in the callous, laissez-faire mindset that spreads infection." Wolf gave me a worried look. I nodded back with confidence. The interviewer continued framing, "As chosen leaders guiding us towards freedom from the disease, what would you say that leadership itself looks like?"

Wolf took a stab, "Well this is a wonderful question. I surely wouldn't have said, before all this happened, that leadership would look like the two of us… two poor, mixed-race teenagers from small town America sneaking out on their parents and jumping trains in the middle of the night."

The reporter smiled and polite laugher rippled through the dispersed crowd. We'd almost forgotten that everyone was watching live.

Wolf went on, "And I still have no idea what it means to be a leader. All I know is that, when I was thrown back in time, in a place where I had a chance to do something to help, to free someone, I felt like I didn't have a choice. It was just wrong, and I couldn't *not* do something about it. I thought, '*To separate ourselves from each other to such an extent as so enslave each other? This must end. We <u>must</u> see each other as human, as equal.*' That's what inspired me to act. Is that being a leader? I don't know. Maybe just not ignoring a solution to a problem sitting right there in front of you is leadership."

A round of applause echoed into the canyons behind us. I beamed. Then I realized the question was coming to me.

The reporter turned and asked, "And you, Cat, what would you say?"

"Well, Wolf's a lot more articulate than I am," I confessed, "I'm not the wordsmith she is. I guess I would just say that sometimes leadership looks different. Sometimes it's the quiet person, doing things quietly alone, who leads."

It was then, in the middle of the news conference, before we had to face any more questions, that we saw them.

Flocks of paper wolves flew in from overhead. Amateur drone pilots had collected and commandeered legions of the brand new drones that had been grown from infected bodies.

They'd fashioned cardboard and newspaper. They'd pasted yellow Post-It notes in homage to my container decorations. They'd reinforced college rule paper. All of it was cut, folded and glued onto mass waves of airborne paper wolves flocking in.

Some of the drone-mounted paper constructions were positioned as if the wolves were jumping mid-flight. Some were in reclining positions. Each was an unmistakable tribute. The paper wolf had become a symbol much larger than itself, or anyone one of us in awe of the wave wafting over our heads at that moment.

The cameras set up for the press conference all turned to cover it. The sky grew dark from it. They buzzed and hummed.

Then a sound started to emanate from the crowd. It was the clever influencer who interviewed us before the conference. She started it.

She cocked her head back to catch the fleets and flocks of paper wolves amassed in the sky. Then she let out a giant,

"HOOOWWWWOOOOOOOOOOOOOOOO!"

She was joined by others. The crowd started to howl. Everyone started howling.

A million or more throats sang in unison, each in their own packs safely clustered away from each other. They harmonized from afar, inspired by my Wolf, in love with our story, in honor of my train car.

20

Wolf's Howl

We had them at the tip of our tongue. Cat and I were using our celebrity. People were having ambitions for collective experiences. They were traveling to join our reunion site like an event or a show. They weren't there to glom onto our celebrity. They weren't there to witness our individual achievement. They were less and less interested in our fame and glory. They just had nowhere else to go. Infections had riddled the world, torn families and decimated friendships. People didn't need an example, a solution, new information, or a hand to hold. They just needed a sign.

The mechanical disease was abating. It was working. Technological bits were dissolving from people's skin. Some units were even breaking apart, with the formerly infected person inside reforming into a healthy human again. It was happening.

We just needed to finish this thing off so it wouldn't rise again. Flat screens, Sega consoles, digital projectors, 3D-scanners, radar screens, heart monitors, and external hard drives were still forming in the place of human bodies. The high tide of the disease was receding. But, if Cat and I didn't rise higher to our occasion, the ocean of traits that kept the cancer alive would rise again.

On the last day of our quarantine, we organized our own press conference. This time CNN, NBC and FoxNews would be joined by frontline reporters from Al Jazeera, Univision, BBC, RT and China Central Television. We halted all other interviews until our demand for a prime time broadcast – shuttering all other transmissions and programming – was met to air our news stream. Friendly relations reached the farthest corners of bloggers and influencers assembled at our reunion site. We tag-teamed bloggers from Mid-east nations with Al Jazeera field reporters. We hooked up right-wing reporters with "underground" beat stories to make them feel like they were uncovering conspiracies. We massaged the egos of Chinese, Russian and North Korean state-run station managers. Representatives from all these factions were surrounding us. We'd been friendly to all. We had only asked for our own privacy at times. But we never shut anyone out. Nearly three weeks of playing ball with influential PR teams from all over the world came to fruition.

Words circling in my head were forming outside my head. I started writing around the fifth day of quarantine. At first it was a long, first-person, non-fiction narrative. I figured no one would want to listen to that. Cat and I were already delivering that content to interviewers. I wanted to write a song but I'm not a great singer and I have no idea how to write (or read) music. I'm not even a poet. It just came out.

I was thinking about Cat, his Dad who left him, and his Dad's ancestors who came from Africa. I was thinking about Amanda Gorman, the 22-year old poet who inspired a nation at a presidential inauguration. I was thinking about Saul Williams, a predecessor who pioneered a genre that would've inspired Ms. Gorman. I was thinking about who would've inspired Mr. Williams: Nikki Giovanni, Maya Angelou, Gil-Scott Heron, The Last Poets and Jacob Lawrence. I traced the line further and further back until I arrived at my friend Harry. I traced the line from Harry, through me, then back to the quagmire of our infections. That's where it came from.

The cameras were ready. It was the largest possible assembly of an international audience, a truly diverse representation of eyes that cut across the boundaries of access. It was at the sharpened tipping point when people were just ready to decide – because history had been changed, and Cat's return was so inspiring – that they needed to change their behavior, band together, end seven years of suffering, and destroy the disease once and for all.

Phones were aimed. TV news cameras were mounted on tripods. Digital cameras were set. Booms and mics were positioned. Lights were on.

We had no other choice but to use the tech to get the word out. It had an intensely counterproductive effect for a few moments before I started. Pockets flared as the symptoms grew worse for those who'd been mildly infected. Wires rooted into stomachs. Skulls mutated into programmable pressure cookers. Chests, stomachs and hips mutated into the monitors and dials of EKG units. Fingers and toes tangled into plugs, adaptors and extension cords.

I hesitated at the prospect, "Cat, maybe this is just going to make things worse".

Cat assured, "Go on, Wolfie. They just need to listen. That's all. Things will calm down… like, darkest before the dawn, and all that, remember?"

"But things were getting better. *Now* look," I pointed to a monitor showing footage of new symptoms.

He reminded me, "That's just a reaction to the tech. You need to start talking. They need to see you – to see a person, not another machine. Step into their frame, Wolfie."

A giant conflagration of recording implements was about to stream my every word across the planet.

I cleared my throat, "Hello. My name is Wolf. I'm an eighteen year old daughter of a Korean immigrant and American factory worker. You've probably heard the rest of my story by now. My love, Cat, and I think we have a cure to end the cancer. The cure is inside all of us. It's inside me. It's inside you. Many of us gathered here, some million or so folks, have found it. I'd like to help more of you find it, if you're willing to bend your ear and listen. It's inside these words that I'm about to deliver. It's in a collection of words, a poem. The poem is called '21 Moons', and it goes like this:

> *It works with common cause*
> *Even if many oppress a few.*
> *It fails to exist because*

A few oppress so many anew.
To just ask, 'Who's on what team?'
End the task, 'Find your own dream.
You get yours, I get mine.
You go your way.
I'll be fine.'

It keeps us parted 'til it's beat.
We can't smash the bug under feet.
The last separation could be dignified
To repair it - that which grows between.
We meet and we re-flare it.
It turns us into screens,
It turns us into drones.
A separation clones
The hate to keep the virus grown.

Cat was long trippin home.
He learned from afar
To atone, not to bar
The connectivity
Sickly skins of circuitry

I learned in packs.
Our paired acts attack
To turn hands back
Of time and the races
My lover cut in spaces.
Separate 'gether, the top of our minds,
Floating two feathers on dove and eagle time.

Match each other's plans.
Agree on one way how

To part in one short span.
Part from the sorrow, part from disease.
'Twenty days plus tomorrow'
Howl it loud, if you please.

The robot cancer grows.
Just part til your skin and kin,
Until there's no more shows
Of more toasters, of more clocks,
Of more smart phones in our wrists,
Of more players,
Of more socks made of wire exist.

No more metal on our spine,
No more copper to and fro,
No more 'vices when we go.
Go the same way. You and me.
Please, today, I say: agree.
To do the same thing,
To band to decree,
'Part, but be waiting.'
Twenty-one moons and you'll see
Twenty-one noons and we'll be
Humans, not machinery.
Just twenty-one sunsets
Until we all are free."

21

Cat's Pur

Wolf finished her poem to a silence. Then they rose to their feet. Grown men wept. Children howled and adults joined them. A harmonizing cry rained down.

Wolf stepped from the mountain of microphones. "It's been exactly twenty-one days, Kitty Cat."

We left our quarantine circles. Her skin came into focus. Her eyes were darker than I remembered. Her hair was silkier, her fingernails narrower. Our hug was cast around the world. Our bodies shook. I couldn't hold her tighter. "We did it Wolfie." I yelled to the camera operators, "NOW PULL THE PLUG!"

Three weeks later, the cancer died. The million or so who'd congregated at our reunion self-selected a quarantine period in solidarity with Wolf and I. Many self-imposed quarantines during those three weeks. They were clear of infection in the days that followed. For those who hadn't started before her poem, they started then, and were clear three weeks later.

Some devices didn't fall apart and return to form. They were too badly infected, or they were never meant to be human in the first place.

For the heavily infected who did come back, the panels of copy machines, guitar amplifiers and stereo receivers were falling apart and dissolving. Apparently I wasn't totally alone up there - even for some of the machines inside my cargo container, human parts regrew and bodies returned. Hoverboards, Segways and e-bikes broke apart in bits as human bodies grew from inside them. Portable electric heaters, generators and solar panels melted down until heads, feet and toes appeared. Microwaves, Keurig's, Alexa's, Google Home devices, programable bread makers, rice cookers, and Yamaha keyboards fell apart with healthy arms and legs emerging in their place.

My Dad never came back. That story never changed. Mom did. She survived the ordeal of being turned into a state-of-the-art 35mm film projector (she was a major classic movie buff).

When we left our reunion site I asked, "Wolfie, what were you telling yourself back there trying to free them from that train?"

"I was so absorbed in the moment without you," she told me, "but you were still there inspiring me to pounce. It was the first time I was doing anything without you. But I just kept asking myself what you'd do. I kept thinking about you, your Dad, and what lead up to where you were."

"I hit a point where the inner cat took over. Like, no one was coming to help me. No one was coming to save me." I sighed, "Like, we're all just on our own, forever."

Wolf admitted, "Now I just feel like I saved the world without you."

Our hands had slowly let go. We were walking on parallel rails. Our eyes stayed down so we wouldn't fall over.

We thought our reunion site had cleared but a woman was screaming, "WOLFIE!!" Wolf's Mom lowered her voice, "My little Wolfie!"

Just like me, her Dad didn't came back, but her Mom did. Wolf ran and buried into her Mom's crook. "How did you do it, mama?"

She answered, "I knew my stray would come back. The pack always reunites." Part of her hadn't finished changing back. AKFASTBOT was still visible in the curved panels receding from her spine. She saw me notice and said, "Right, Kitty Cat?"

I rewound my time with BreakfastBot, trying to remember if I'd ever treated the machine poorly. I admitted, "I think I only called you a 'he.' I thought you were a boy."

"Well I don't remember thinking," Wolf's Mom radiated warmly, "But I do remember feeling. And I remember a good feeling."

It only took three weeks once the public was persuaded to cure it themselves, without hand-outs, roll-outs or government intervention.

Wolf reflected as walked with her Mom, "365 weeks could've ended in 3. It's just so sad."

I rolled my eyes, "What - like, we could've avoided the whole thing? Like it was all just in the mind?"

Wolf moaned, "Right - like, it was just so easy to do in."

The End

"The Cure for Robot Cancer"
By Uncle Mikey

Illustrations
by Michael Gipson Leavitt
Acrylic & marker on paper

www.ingramcontent.com/pod-product-compliance
Lightning Source LLC
Chambersburg PA
CBHW051248150726
48001CB00019B/1726